PENGUIN MODERN CLASSICS

THE FRONTENAC MYSTERY

François Mauriac was born in Bordeaux on 11 October
1885. He was a brilliant pupil, studying first with the
Marianites at Caudéran, then at a lycée, and finally at
the Faculté des Lettres in Bordeaux and the École des
Chartes in Paris. He started writing early and his poems
appeared in the *Revue du temps présent*; in 1907 his
literary career began with a book of poetry, *L'Adieu à
l'adolescence* and a novel, *L'Enfant chargé de chaines*.

In 1914 he married and was then mobilized to serve in
the First World War with the Auxiliary Medical Squad
in Thessalonica.

In 1932 François Mauriac became President of the
Society for 'Gens de Lettres'; in 1933 he was elected a
Member of the French Academy; and in 1936 he was
made a Commander of the Legion of Honour. He
wrote plays, poetry, biographies, criticism and some
articles for the press; his main achievement lay in the
novel, and in recognition of this he was awarded the
Grand Prix du Roman for *Le Désert de l'amour* (1925)
and in 1952 received the Nobel Prize for Literature. He
died in 1970.

Penguin also publish *Thérèse* and *The Knot of Vipers*.

François Mauriac

THE
FRONTENAC
MYSTERY

Translated by Gerard Hopkins

PENGUIN BOOKS

Penguin Books Ltd, Harmondsworth, Middlesex, England
Viking Penguin Inc., 40 West 23rd Street, New York, New York 10010, U.S.A.
Penguin Books Australia Ltd, Ringwood, Victoria, Australia
Penguin Books Canada Ltd, 2801 John Street, Markham, Ontario, Canada L3R 1B4
Penguin Books (N.Z.) Ltd, 182–190 Wairau Road, Auckland 10, New Zealand

First published in France as *Le Mystère Frontenac* 1933
This translation first published in Great Britain by Eyre & Spottiswoode 1951
Published in Penguin Books 1986

Printed and bound in Great Britain by
Cox & Wyman Ltd, Reading
Typeset in Bembo

Comme un fruit suspendu dans l'ombre du feuillage,
Mon destin s'est formé dans l'épaisseur des bois.
J'ai grandi, recouvert d'un chaleur sauvage,
Et le vent qui rompait le tissu de l'ombrage
Me découvrit le ciel pour la première fois.
Les faveurs de nos dieux m'ont touché dès l'enfance;
Mes plus jeunes regards ont aimé les forêts,
Et mes plus jeunes pas ont suivi le silence
Qui m'entrainait bien loin dans l'ombre et les secrets.

MAURICE DE GUÉRIN

PART ONE

I

XAVIER FRONTENAC glanced shyly at his sister-in-law. She was sitting very upright on the chair which she had drawn to the fire. She made no use of its back, and she was knitting. He could see that she was annoyed, and tried to remember what he had said at dinner. His remarks, in retrospect, seemed to him to have been completely innocent of offence.

His eyes were focused on the great bed with its twisted columns, in which eight years before, his brother, Michel Frontenac, had died with such agonizing slowness. In imagination he could still see the head thrown back, the massive neck, the unshaven stubble, and the cloud of June flies which he had been unable to keep from settling on the sweat-covered face. Nowadays, they might have tried trepanning. Michel might have been saved, might be with them now. . . . Xavier could not take his eyes from the bed, from the walls, though it was not in this room that his brother had died. A week after the funeral Blanche Frontenac, and her five children, had left their home in the rue Vital-Carles, and taken refuge on the third floor of the house in the rue de Cursol, where her mother, Madame Arnaud-Miqueu lived. But the old blue curtains, with their patterning of yellow flowers, still hung before the windows and around the bed. The chest-of-drawers and the wardrobe still faced one another as in the old room. On the mantelpiece the bronze statuette of Faith still stood – a woman in a high-necked, long-sleeved dress. Only the lamp was different. Madame Frontenac had bought one of an improved design, much admired by all the members of the family: an alabaster column topped by a glass container in which a broad wick, like a tape-worm, lay soaking. The flame sprouted a cluster of incandescent petals. The shade was a jumble of cream-coloured lace, adorned with bunches of artificial violets.

This marvel served as a lure for the children. They were always hungry for reading. In honour of Uncle Xavier, they were allowed to stay up until half-past nine. The two eldest, Jean-Louis and José, had wasted not a moment before getting down to their books – the two first volumes of Alexandre de Lamothe's *Camisards*. Lying at full length on the floor, with their fingers stuffed in their ears, they were deep in the story, and lost to all else. Xavier Frontenac could see nothing but their round, cropped heads, their projecting ears, their big knees, all scratched and scarred, their grubby legs, and their nailed boots with the laces tied in knots.

Yves, the youngest, whom no one would have thought was ten years old, was not reading. He sat perched on a stool at his mother's side, rubbing his face against her knees, as though trying, instinctively, to get back into the body from which he had emerged. He was thinking that between tomorrow's black-board, between Monsieur Roche's German lesson, and going to bed, a whole blessed night would intervene. 'I may die – I may fall ill' . . . He had deliberately forced himself to over-eat of every dish.

Behind the bed, the two little girls, Danièle and Marie, sat learning their catechism. Their uncontrollable and stifled laughter could be plainly heard. Even at home the atmosphere of the Sacred Heart isolated them. They could think of nothing but their mistresses and their school-friends, and, quite often, lay talking in their twin beds until as late as eleven o'clock.

Xavier Frontenac looked at the bullet-heads gathered at his feet, at Michel's children, at the last of the Frontenacs. Lawyer and man of business though he was, he felt his throat contract.

His heart beat quicker. This cluster of flesh and blood was his brother's legacy. Being, as he was, indifferent to anything of a religious nature, he would have hated to think that there was even the hint of a mystery in his feelings. The particular characteristics of his nephews meant nothing to him. Jean-Louis was a schoolboy brimming over with life and intelligence; but, had he been no more than a brainless young animal, his uncle would not have loved him less. What gave them value in his eyes had nothing to do with individual qualities.

"Half-past nine," exclaimed Blanche Frontenac; "time for bed – and don't forget to say your prayers."

On the evenings when Uncle Xavier was present, prayers were not said in common.

"Don't take your books upstairs with you."

"How far have you got?" – asked Jean-Louis of his brother.

"I'm just at the bit where Jean Cavalier . . ."

The little girls presented their damp foreheads to their uncle. Yves hung back.

"You *will* come and tuck me up, mamma, won't you?"

"Not if you set such store by it."

The sickliest of her boys looked back at her from the door with an imploring expression. His socks were barely visible above his shoes. His thin little face was all ears. His left lid drooped and almost completely hid the eye.

When the children had gone, Xavier Frontenac continued to observe his sister-in-law. She was still on the defensive. In what way had he wounded her? He had spoken of women who had a strong sense of duty, women of whom she was typical. He did not realize that the widow found praise of that sort peculiarly exasperating. The poor man was for ever, with a sort of heavy insistence, extolling the splendours of sacrifice, declaring that there was nothing lovelier in the world than the faith-

ful devotion of a woman to her dead husband, than her
absorption in her children. It was only in terms of the young
Frontenacs that she existed for him at all. It never occurred to
him that she might be a young and lonely woman, still capable
of sadness and despair. He was not interested in her personal
destiny. So long as she did not re-marry, so long as she gave
herself to the bringing up of Michel's children, he cared little
what might happen to her. That was what Blanche could never
forgive. Not that she felt any regrets. On the very threshold of
her widowhood she had taken stock of her sacrifice and
accepted it. Nothing could have made her go back on her
decision. But she was a very religious woman, somewhat
scrupulous and arid in her piety, and it would never have
occurred to her that without God she could have found the
strength to live as she had determined to do, for she was young
and ardent, and her heart was hungry. If, on this particular
evening, Xavier had had eyes to see he might well have felt
a moment's pity – seeing the litter of books on the floor, and
all the jumble of the abandoned nest – for this tragic mother
with the black eyes, and the sick, lined face, in whom the traces
of a former beauty still warred with wrinkles and approaching
age. Her greying, rather untidy hair gave her the neglected
look of a woman who has nothing to look forward to. The
black bodice, buttoned down the front, drew attention to her
thin shoulders and sagging breast. Everything about her told
of fatigue, of that exhaustion felt by a mother whose children
are eating her alive. What she wanted was not to be admired
and pitied, but to be understood. Her brother-in-law's blind
indifference so angered her that she became violent and unjust.
As soon as he was not with her, she was overcome with remorse, and beat her breast: but her good resolutions were not
proof against the presence of that inexpressive face, of that
little man with the blind eyes, for whom she scarcely existed

at all, who would gladly have wiped her altogether from his mind.

There was the sound of a small voice. Yves was calling. He could not control his terror, yet dreaded lest he might be heard.

"Oh, that child!"

Blanche Frontenac got up, but went first to the two older boys. They were already fast asleep, with scapulars clutched in their grubby hands. She tucked them in, and, with her thumb, traced a cross upon their foreheads. Then she went into the girls' room. A light was showing under the door. As soon as they heard their mother they extinguished it. Madame Frontenac re-lit the candle. On the table between the two beds some sections of an orange were lying on a doll's plate. Another plate contained nibbled chocolate and a few crumbs of biscuit. The little imps were hiding under the sheets, and Blanche could see no more of them than plaits of hair tied with faded ribbon.

"No dessert . . . and I shall make a note in your conduct book that you have been disobedient."

She removed the remains of the "midnight feast". But, as she closed the door, she heard a little splutter of laughter behind her. In the room next door, Yves was lying wide awake. He alone was allowed to have a night-light. His shadow showed upon the wall, the head looking enormous, the neck no bigger than a flower's stalk. He was sitting up in bed, and crying. He buried his face in his mother's dress, so as not to hear her reproaches. She had meant to scold him, but could hear the wild beating of his heart, could feel against her body the pressure of his skinny ribs and shoulder-blades. At such times, made aware of the almost endless possibilities of suffering in the small creature before her, she was conscious of something very like terror, and fell to comforting him.

"My little silly . . . my little donkey. How many times have I told you that you are not alone? Jesus lives in the hearts of little children. When you are frightened, you should call on him, and he will comfort you."

"No, he won't, because I have committed terrible sins. . . . It's different with you, mummy: when you're there, I know that you are there . . . I can touch you and feel you. . . . Oh, do stay a little longer!"

She told him that he must go to sleep, that Uncle Xavier was waiting for her. She assured him that he was in a state of grace. There was nothing about her little boy, she said. that she did not know. He grew calmer. From time to time, but at long intervals, a sob shook him.

Madame Frontenac tip-toed from the room.

II

A S she entered the room, Xavier Frontenac gave a start.
"I think I must have dropped off . . . I find these tours of inspection round the family estates rather tiring."

"Well, you have no one to blame but yourself" – there was a note of bitterness in Blanche's voice: "why on earth must you choose to live in Angoulême, so far from all of us? You could quite easily have sold your practice after Michel died. It would have been the most natural thing in the world for you to have made your home in Bordeaux, and taken his place in the business. . . . I know, of course, that we hold the majority of the shares, but the man who really runs it is Dussol,

Michel's partner. Not that I have anything against him: he's a thoroughly decent man: still, the fact remains that because of you, my boys will find it increasingly difficult to fit into the family concern."

She realized, even while she was speaking, how unfair it was of her to blame her brother-in-law. His failure to defend himself amazed her. Not one word of protest did he utter, but sat with hanging head as though she had laid her finger on some hidden wound. It would have been so easy for him to have made a case for himself, to have reminded her how, after old Frontenac's death, which had followed hard on the heels of Michel's, he had renounced all his own holdings in the property, and made them over to the children. Blanche, at first, had thought that he had done so in order to free himself from the tiresome necessity of keeping a watchful eye on the estates. But so far was this from being the case, that he had offered to "run" the vineyards, in which he had ceased to have any lot or part, solely in the interests of his nephews. Every other Friday, no matter what the state of the weather, he left Angoulême round about three o'clock, caught a train at Bordeaux which landed him at Langon, where either the victoria or the brougham, according as the day was hot or cold, was waiting for him at the station. About two kilometres from the little town, just before reaching Preignac, on the main road, the carriage turned in at a gate, and Xavier caught the bitter and familiar smell of ancient box.

Two wings, built by their great-grandfather, completely ruined the façade of the eighteenth-century monastery which had been the home of so many generations of Frontenacs. He climbed the curved entrance-steps, and at once his nose was assailed by the peculiar odour which winter damp imparts to old hangings. Though his parents had survived their eldest son for only a short while, the house had remained open. The gardener was still living in one of the cottages on the estate. A coachman, a cook, and a housemaid had stayed on to look after Félicia, old Frontenac's youngest sister, who had been "backward" from birth (it was said that the doctor had been too vigorous in his manipulation of the forceps).

Xavier's first concern, on these occasions, was to look for his aunt. In fine weather, he would find her dawdling under the glass canopy over the porch; in winter, drowsing by the kitchen fire. He showed no fear of the permanently upturned eyes, of which only the veined whites were visible, of the twisted mouth, of the strange fluff of youthful beard around her chin. He kissed the old lady on the forehead with tender respect, for the name of this monstrous apparition was Félicia Frontenac. She was a member of the family, his father's sister, the sole remaining representative of her generation. When the gong sounded for dinner, he approached the poor, mindless creature, gave her his arm, led her into the dining-room, sat her down opposite him, and fastened a napkin round her neck. It was doubtful whether he even noticed the food dribbling from the horrible mouth, or heard her eructations. The meal over, he led her out with the same ceremony, and handed her over to the care of old Jeannette.

Left to himself, he made his way to the immense room in the wing which looked out on to the river and the slope of the hill, the room which, for so many years, he and Michel had shared. In winter-time a fire was kept burning there all day long. In fine weather, the windows were left open, and he could look out at the vineyards and the pastures. A nightingale ceased its song in the catalpa tree where nightingales had always been. . . . Michel, as a young man, used to get up in order to listen to them. In imagination, Xavier could see the white, lanky figure leaning out over the garden. Half asleep, he would call out to him: "Come back to bed, Michel: it's silly to run the risk of catching a cold!'' For a bare handful of days and nights the flowering vines would smell of mignonette. . . .

He opened a volume of Balzac, in an attempt to rid himself of ghosts. But the book slipped from his hands. He thought of Michel, and tears came into his eyes.

Always, at eight o'clock next morning, the carriage was waiting, and he spent the day visiting his nephews' land. From Cernès in the marsh, where the grape crop gives a heavy wine, he went to Respide, on the outskirts of Saint-Croix-aux-Monts, where the vines are as good as in Sauterne: then, over towards Couamères, on the Casteljaloux road, where cattle were raised, but always at a dead loss.

Everywhere he went he had to make enquiries, study account books, smell out the tricks and cunning of peasants who would have got the better of him but for the anonymous letters which he found each week in his post. Finally, having done his duty by the children, he returned to the house so worn out that, after a hurried meal, he went straight to bed. He thought that he was sleepy, but sleep would not come. The dying fire woke him with its flicker of low flames on the ceiling and the mahogany chairs – or, in springtime, the night-ingale to which the ghost of Michel still listened.

Next morning, being Sunday, Xavier got up late, put on a starched shirt, a pair of striped trousers, a short jacket, made of cloth or alpaca, narrow, pointed button-boots, a bowler or a straw hat, and made his way to the cemetery. The custodian, seeing him approach, made him a sign of welcome. Xavier did his best, with endless tips, to win the man's favour in the interests of the dead. That was the most he could do for them. Sometimes his pointed boots stuck in the mud, sometimes they were covered in dust from the cinder paths. The sanctified earth was a maze of mole-runs. He, a living Frontenac, stood uncovered in the presence of all the Frontenacs who had to dust returned. There was nothing he could say, nothing he could do. Like most of his contemporaries, obscure and eminent alike, he was walled up in his materialism, his determinism, prisoner of a universe that was infinitely more limited than Aristotle's had ever been. He stood, holding his bowler in his left hand while, with his right, just to keep himself in countenance in this city of the dead, he plucked a few overblown roses.

In the afternoon, the five o'clock express took him back to Bordeaux. After buying some cakes and some sweets, he rang his sister-in-law's doorbell. There was a sound of scampering footsteps in the passage. The children cried: "It's Uncle Xavier!" Small hands scrabbled competitively at the latch. Nephews and nieces flung themselves between his legs, eager for parcels.

"I'm sorry, Xavier" – Blanche Frontenac was saying (her second thoughts were always kindly) : "you must forgive me – I'm not always mistress of my nerves. . . . You are a model uncle. Of that I need no reminder. . . ."

As always, he seemed not to hear, or, rather, to attach no importance to, what she was saying. With his hands tucked under his coat-tails, he paced the room. With a round and anxious eye he murmured that it was "no good doing things by halves. . . ." Once again the certainty was borne in on Blanche that she had deeply wounded him. She did what she could to reassure him. There was no reason at all, she said, why he should live in Bordeaux if he preferred to stay on in Angoulême, or concern himself with the sale of timber, if he had a liking for the law. She added:

"I know that your practice is small, and does not really take up all your time . . ."

Again, a look of fear came into his eyes, as though he were

terrified lest she might read his secrets. She invariably tried hard to win him over, though the most he ever gave her was a feigned attention. She would have been overjoyed had he confided in her: but there was a wall between them. To her he never spoke of the past, nor, especially, of Michel. He had his memories, but they belonged to him alone. They could be shared with nobody. He honoured her as the mother and protector of the last of the Frontenacs, but regarded her as a member, only, of the Arnaud-Miqueu family, as a woman of great gifts, but, for all that, an outsider. Disappointed, and a prey once more to irritation, she held her peace. Why wouldn't he go to bed? He sat, resting his elbow on his skinny legs, poking the fire as though there were nobody else in the room.

"By the by," he said suddenly: "Jeannette asked me for some patterns of material. It seems that Aunt Félicia needs a new spring dress."

"Ah " – said Blanche – "Aunt Félicia!" Then, prompted by some devil –

"It's high time," she added, "that you and I had a serious talk about Aunt Félicia."

She had won his attention at last. The globular eyes came to rest on her face. What hare was she going to start now? She was so touchy, always so ready to take the offensive, that one could never be sure.

"You must admit that it is scarcely reasonable to pay the wages of three servants and a gardener just to look after a poor, half-witted creature who would be far better tended, and, which is perhaps more important, far more efficiently supervised, in a Home. . . ."

"A Home? . . . Aunt Félicia in a Home?"

She had certainly succeeded in breaking down his reserve! His mottled cheeks, from being red grew purple.

"So long as I live" – he exclaimed in a high-pitched voice –

"Aunt Félicia will never be asked to leave our family house. My father's wishes will be carried out to the letter. He was never separated from his sister. . . ."

"Oh, come now! He used to leave Preignac every Monday morning, give the whole week to business, and not get back from Bordeaux until Saturday evening. It was your poor mother, unaided, who had to cope with Aunt Félicia!"

"And she was only too pleased to do so! . . . You know nothing about our family attitude in such matters. . . . It would never have occurred to her even to wonder . . . Félicia was her husband's sister. . . ."

"That's what *you* think . . . but the poor dear used to pour herself out to me, used to tell me of the long years of solitude when she had had to live in unrelieved intimacy with an idiot. . . ."

Xavier burst out in a fury:

"I refuse to believe that she ever complained; least of all, that she complained to you. . . ."

"You forget that my mother-in-law regarded me as one of the family. She was fond of me. In her eyes I was never a stranger."

"Would you mind leaving my parents out of this?" – he broke in acidly. "Where family duty is in question, the Frontenacs have never considered money. If you find it too much of a burden to defray half the expenses of the Preignac house, I am prepared to shoulder the whole cost myself. You seem to forget, too, that Aunt Félicia had certain rights under our grandfather's will, rights of which my parents took no account when the estate came to be broken up among the heirs. My poor father never bothered his head about the law. . . ."

Blanche, stung to the quick, made no further attempt to hold back what she had been keeping in reserve ever since the argument started:

"I may not be a Frontenac, but I consider it to be my children's duty to contribute to their great-aunt's maintenance, and even to assure the continuance of a ridiculously expensive style of living which she is in no condition to enjoy. Since that is your whim, I bow to it. But what I will not have" – she went on, raising her voice – "is that they should be made the victims of that whim, and that because of you their future happiness should be endangered. . . ."

She broke off. The silence that followed was a carefully calculated effect. He could not, for the life of him, see what she was getting at.

"Aren't you ever afraid of what people may say about her? Has it never occurred to you that she may be regarded as a congenital lunatic?"

"Really! – everyone knows that the poor woman's head was crushed by the doctor's forceps."

"Everyone at Preignac, between 1840 and 1860, knew it: but if you think that the present generation have such long memories, you are very much mistaken . . . No, my dear Xavier: it is time you plucked up courage to look your responsibilities in the face. You insist that Aunt Félicia shall continue to live in the home of her fathers – though, in fact, she makes use of little more than the kitchen – and shall be looked after by three servants who are free to do exactly as they like. For all we know, they may make her life a misery. . . . But it is your brother's children who will suffer for all this when they reach the marrying age. They may well find that all doors are closed to them. . . ."

Blanche's victory was complete – so complete, that she began to feel afraid. Xavier Frontenac had the look of a man who has been utterly crushed. But there was nothing factitious about her anxiety. The idea that Aunt Félicia might be a source of great embarrassment to the children, was of no recent birth.

The threat, however, was not immediate, and she had, perhaps, exaggerated. . . .

Xavier was too honest not to admit defeat:

"I fear that that had never occurred to me. My poor Blanche, where the children are concerned I am terribly thoughtless."

He began to pace up and down the room. His knees were slightly bent, and he dragged his feet. Blanche's anger had evaporated no less quickly than it had formed. Her triumph was already making her feel guilty. There was still time, she protested: everything could be put right. No one in Bordeaux even knew of Aunt Félicia's existence. She wouldn't live for ever, and would soon be forgotten. Seeing that Xavier was still gloomy, she added:

"A great many people think that she had a fall when she was a child. That, in fact, is the general view. . . . I don't believe she has been regarded as an actual lunatic. But, later on, she might be. . . . Our duty is to avert a possible danger. . . . You mustn't let yourself get into a state about it, my poor dear. You know how prone I am to be carried away, how I always exaggerate. . . . I'm made like that."

His breath was coming in little gasping intakes. Both his father and his mother had died, she remembered, of heart trouble. ('I might be the death of him.') He had sat down again by the fire, all hunched in his chair. In an effort to control her thoughts she closed her eyes. Their long, dark lashes softened the hard lines of the embittered face. He did not guess that the woman beside him was humbling herself, was suffering agonies because of her inability to discipline her feelings. The confused muttering of a child, caught in a dream, broke the silence of the room. It was time, said Xavier, to go to bed: he would think over what they had been talking about. She assured him that they had plenty of time, that no decision need be taken immediately.

"I cannot agree with you there: we must act quickly. After all, what is at stake is the children's future."

"You let yourself worry too much," she said briskly: "I know I am always blaming and criticizing you, but, for all that, I do realize that there are not many such uncles in the world. . . ."

He made a gesture which might have meant – "you don't know . . ." Most certainly he had got something on his conscience, but what it was she could not imagine.

A few minutes later, kneeling at her evening prayer, she tried in vain to bring her mind to bear upon the familiar words. When Xavier next came she really would make an effort to find out more about him. But it wouldn't be easy, because he so rarely gave himself away to anybody, and never to her. . . . She found it impossible to concentrate. It was high time for her to be in bed and asleep: tomorrow morning she must be up early, otherwise José, her youngest, would never do a scrap of preparation before starting for school. He was as regularly at the bottom of his class as Jean-Louis was at the top. It wasn't that he lacked the intelligence, the quickness, of the other two, but only that he seemed to have a positive genius for letting his mind wander, for not listening to what was being said to him. He was one of those boys on whom words make no impact, in whom absent-mindedness ranks almost as a gift; one of those boys who go mentally flaccid when grown-up persons try to get anything out of them, who sit over their torn school-books and smudged notes in a mood of heavy listlessness. Their minds, nimble enough in other respects, are far away among the tall Whitsun grasses, along the river bank, intent on crayfish. Blanche knew that for three-quarters of an hour she would struggle in vain with this sleepy child of hers, who would be as incapable of concentrating, as empty of thought, and even of life, as an abandoned chrysalis.

Would she, when the children had gone, bother about breakfast? Yes, of course she would: no purpose could be served by starving herself. . . . How, after the way she had behaved this evening to her brother-in-law, could she take Communion? . . . Then there would be the Charity Organization, and, after that, her meeting with the architect to discuss the house in the rue St. Catherine. And, of course, she must find time to visit her poor. She must remember, too, to look in at Potine's to arrange for a parcel of groceries to go to the Rescue Home. I am particularly devoted to this Charity . . . In the evening, after dinner, when the children had gone to bed, she would run downstairs to see her mother. Her sister would be there, with her husband. Perhaps Aunt Adila, too, or the Abbé Mellon, the senior priest of the parish. . . . There are women who know what it is to be loved. . . . Now that she had got all these children no one would ever want to marry her unless for her money. . . . That was not quite true. . . . She had every reason to believe that she was still attractive. . . . There had been incidents – but she mustn't think of them. But hadn't she, perhaps, begun to think of them a little? . . . Above all, none of this scrupulosity. There could be no question of her depriving her children of any part of herself, however small. . . . There was nothing meritorious in that decision, it was just the way she was made. . . . She was so sure that they would pay in their flesh for any evil action of hers . . . and yet, that was a baseless fear, as she very well knew. She was condemned for ever to sacrifice herself for her children. The knowledge of that had been a cause of much suffering. . . . A woman with nothing to look forward to . . . I am a woman with nothing to look forward to . . . She pressed her hands to her eyes, and drew her fingers down her face . . . must really make an appointment with the dentist . . .

A voice called to her. Yves again! She tip-toed to his room.

He was asleep, but restless. He had thrown off his blankets.
One brown, emaciated leg was hanging over the side of the
bed. She covered him up and tucked him in. He turned his
face to the wall, muttering uneasily. She touched his forehead
and his neck, thinking that he might be feverish.

III

UNCLE XAVIER turned up regularly, every other Sunday. But his sister-in-law came no nearer to discovering
his secret. His reappearances were, for the children, no
less to be counted upon than the monthly whole holiday, than
the weekly Communion, than the recurrent "Essay", and the
reading over of Friday's notes. He was a fixed star in the sky
of childhood, his movements so adjusted to a clockwork pre-
cision, that nothing unusual, it seemed, could possibly interrupt
their sequence. Blanche might have been tempted to believe
that she was dreaming, had it not been that his silences,
his air of absorption, his restlessness, his unseeing stare, and the
puckered expression on his round face (as though some fixed
idea were working in his mind) reminded her of the time when
she, too, had been going through a crisis of scruple. This
deeply religious woman could detect in the brother-in-law
to whom religion meant nothing, the symptoms of that same
ailment of which Father de Nole had cured her. She knew
that trouble all too well, and would, if she could, have reassured him. But he gave her no chance of coming to grips.
Still, she had, blessedly and all unexpectedly, reached a point
at which she could, at least, be sure that she no longer irritated

him. Far less than formerly did they get on one another's nerves. Did he realize the extent of her efforts? She, who once had been so jealous of her authority, now asked his advice on everything that had to do with the children. Did he think it would be a good thing to buy a saddle-horse for Jean-Louis, who was the best rider in the school. Ought she to make Yves take riding-lessons, in spite of his fear of horses? Would it be advisable to let José become a boarder?

Fires were no longer necessary, nor even lamps. The only place in the whole house which remained dark was the corridor, up and down which, for a few minutes before dinner, Blanche would walk, saying her Rosary, with Yves at her heels, holding up her dress with two hands, lost in a dream of magnificence which he would share with no one. The air was filled with the chirruping of swifts. The noise of the trams in the Cours d'Alsace made it impossible to hear oneself speak. The ships' sirens seemed to bring the harbour to their very door. The heat, said Blanche, would melt the children's brains. They invented idiotic games, such as staying in the dining-room when dinner was over, with their napkins on their heads, then hiding away in some obscure corner and rubbing noses – which they called playing at "Communities".

One Saturday in June, when Blanche had long given up thinking about Uncle Xavier's secret, the key to it was suddenly put into her hand. Light shone suddenly from the most unexpected of quarters. The children had retired to bed, and she had gone down, as usual, to see her mother. After passing through the dining-room where the table had not yet been cleared, and a strong scent of strawberries hung on the air, she had opened the door of the small drawing-room. Madame Arnaud-Miqueu was sitting in a leather armchair which she completely filled. She called to her daughter, and kissed her with the almost ravenous intensity which was habitual with her. Blanche could see on the balcony her brother-in-law Caussade, her sister, and the huge bulk of Aunt Adila, Madame Arnaud-Miqueu's sister-in-law. They were laughing and talking at the tops of their voices, and would have been audible to all the neighbours, had it not been that everyone within hearing distance was being equally clamorous. Down in the street some boys were singing:

> "*Et l'enfant disait au soldat:*
> *Sentinelle, ne tirez pas*
> *C'est un oiseau qui vient de France!*"

Aunt Adila caught sight of her:

"This is no place for you, Blanche, my dear!"

Caussade shouted above the din of the trams:

"I was hoping you'd come. . . . I've got a piece of news for you, a real gem. . . . Keep a tight hold on yourself, you'll never guess!"

"Come on, Alfred, out with it!" – broke in his wife: " she's given it up as a bad job."

"The fact is, my dear, I happened to be appearing yesterday in a case at Angoulême, and it came to my knowledge that your Monsieur Xavier Frontenac is quite openly and blatantly keeping a woman . . . what d'you say to that?"

His wife interrupted him: if he wasn't careful, he'd frighten Blanche, and get her all worked up!

"It's nothing to worry about. No fear of his ruining his nephews. From what I can hear, the poor creature of his choice is scarcely living in what might be called guilty luxury."

Blanche cut him short with the driest of dry comments. She was quite easy on that score, she said, and, in any case, Xavier Frontenac's private life was none of her business – or of theirs.

"See, she's gone all hoity-toity: I told you she would."

"She bullies him like anything herself, but as soon as anybody else says a word, she's up in arms!"

Blanche protested that there was no question of her being what they called "up in arms". Since Xavier, unfortunately for himself, was completely devoid of religious feelings, she couldn't see what there was to stop him from behaving just exactly as he liked.

The voices became less strident. Alfred Caussade, in order to calm his sister-in-law's fears, explained that Xavier Frontenac was an almost legendary figure in Angoulême, where the meanness with which he treated his lady-friend had made him a positive laughing-stock. There was no need for Blanche to lose a moment's sleep. The poor woman earned her living by doing odd jobs of sewing, and he wouldn't hear of her giving up her work. He had furnished a room for her on the cheap, and paid her rent. That was the full extent of his generosity. The thing was a public scandal . . . at which point, Alfred stopped, considerably abashed. Blanche, who was quite unperturbed by dramatic situations, had folded up her work and risen from her chair. She kissed Madame Arnaud-Miqueu, and left the room without addressing a word to her embarrassed relatives. The spirit of the Frontenacs had taken complete possession of her, so that she shook like a Pythian priestess. When she got upstairs, her hand was trembling so violently, that she could scarcely put the key in the lock.

She had come back a good two hours earlier than usual, and it was still daylight. She found the three boys squatting at the window in their nightgowns. They were spitting on the sill and rubbing away at the moist patch with an apricot stone. The object of this proceeding was to wear down the two sides of the stone until it was thin enough to pierce, after which the kernel could be extracted with a needle. If they went on long enough their labours would be rewarded with a whistle, though it never functioned as such, and was always, eventually, eaten. They were amazed at the mildness of their mother's scolding, and scampered away like rabbits. Blanche Frontenac's mind was entirely occupied with the thought of Xavier. She would be seeing him on the next evening, which was one of his regular Sundays. She conjured up a picture of him as he must be at this moment, alone in the huge dead house at Preignac.

On that same evening, Xavier Frontenac had spent a short while sitting under the glass awning. But the heat in the vineyards had been intense, and he was afraid of catching a chill. He wandered about for a moment or two in the hall, and then decided to go upstairs. Far more than the rainy nights of winter, when the fire kept him company and tempted him to read, did he dread these June twilights, "Michel's evenings". In the old days he had laughed at Michel because of his mania for quoting Hugo in and out of season. But now, some of those quotations, rich with the modulations of that loved voice, came back into his mind. He must remember them, so as to hear again his brother's monotonous and muted tones. And so it was that this evening, close to the open window, with the river invisible beyond, Xavier recited to himself, with varying intonation, as though seeking some particular note, some special harmony:

Nature au front serein, comme vous oubliez!

The meadows were strident. As always, the darkness was loud with the croaking of frogs, with laughter, and with the barking of dogs. Leaning from the window, the lawyer from Angoulême spoke aloud, as though each word were being whispered in his ear:

A peine un char lointain glisse dans l'ombre, écoute. . . . Tout dort et se repose et l'arbre de la route. . . . Secoue au vent du soir le poussière du jour. . . .

He turned his back on the window, lit a cheap cigarette, and, as his habit was, began to shuffle up and down the room, with the bottom of his trouser-leg caught between ankle and slipper. He was, he kept saying to himself, betraying Michel in the persons of his children. He chewed at the cud of an old remorse. When he had taken his Law Finals in Bordeaux, he had already been acquainted with this woman. Even in those days she had been shop-soiled, and there had been little in age between them. Why she had had such influence over him he did not seek to discover. In order to answer that question he would have had to probe the mystery of his shyness and his phobias, of his ineffectiveness and of his morbid anxieties. She was a kindly creature with a strong maternal instinct, and she did not laugh at him. In that, perhaps, lay the secret of her power.

Even while Michel was still living, Xavier had accepted the irregular relationship with anything but a light heart. Strictness in morals was traditional in the Frontenac family, and the product not so much of religion as of a republican and peasant past. Neither Xavier's grandfather nor his father could endure dirty talk, and the highly reprehensible domesticities of Uncle Péloueyre, Madame Frontenac's elderly bachelor brother, whose family had inherited the estate of Bourideys, in Les Landes, had always been regarded as a crying scandal. Gossip had it that he used to receive his paramour at Bourideys, in the very house where his parents had died, and that she used to have the effrontery to let herself be seen on the front-door step, at eleven o'clock in the morning, wearing a pink wrap, with nothing on her feet, and her hair hanging down her back. It was in her room in Bordeaux that Uncle Péloueyre had died on the very same day that he had gone into town to make a will in her favour. It gave Xavier the horrors to think that he was following in the old man's footsteps, that he was con-

tinuing, without meaning to, the same tradition of dissipation.
. . . He only hoped that the family would never know anything about it, would never discover his shameful secret! Fear
that they might do so had been behind his decision to buy a
practice at some little distance from Bordeaux. He had hoped
that the silence of Angoulême might close about his private
life.

When Michel died, the family had left him no time to
brood over his sorrow. His parents, who were still living, and
Blanche, had forced him from his condition of dazed misery.
They made it quite clear to him what the family had decided.
It "went without saying" that he would sell his practice, leave
Angoulême, and take Michel's place in the business. Xavier
protested in vain that he knew nothing whatever about timber.
They assured him that Arthur Dussol, his dead brother's
partner, would be there to help him. All the same, he put up
a desperate struggle. The idea of giving up Joséfa was more
than he could bear, and if they settled down together in
Bordeaux, the secret would be public property in next to no
time. He would be sure to run into Blanche and the children
when he was out walking with her on his arm. . . . The very
thought of such an appalling contretemps made him turn pale.
Now that he had become his nephews' guardian it was more
than ever important that the scandal of his private life should
be concealed. After all, with Dussol in charge of the business
there was little likelihood of the children suffering financially,
for most of the shares were in Frontenac hands. All that
mattered to Xavier was that his manner of life should not be
made known. He stuck to his point. For the first time in his
life he set himself up against his father, who was already at
death's door.

But even after the business difficulties were settled, Xavier
had found it impossible to recover his peace of mind. He could

not quietly resign himself to his grief. Remorse still gnawed at him – the same remorse as now set him pacing this childhood's room, between his own bed and the one on which he could still, in imagination, see Michel lying. The family property must come to Michel's children: to keep even a penny of it from them would be tantamount to theft, but it so happened that he had promised Joséfa to deposit in her name on each successive first of January, for the next ten years, the sum of ten thousand francs. It was an understood thing that this should be the sum total of his responsibility, except that, during his life-time, he should continue to pay her rent, and allow her a monthly sum of three hundred francs. By skimping himself (his avarice was a standing joke in Angoulême) he managed to save twenty-five thousand francs a year, but of this only fifteen thousand went to his nephews. He was regularly stealing – so he put it to himself – ten thousand francs each year from them, to say nothing of what he was paying currently to Joséfa. It was true, no doubt, that he had surrendered all claims to profits from the estate, and that, after all, everyone is free to do what he likes with his income: all the same, there did exist a secret law, an obscure law, a Frontenac law, the over-riding claims of which he admitted without so much as questioning its justice. He was an old bachelor, and he held what money he had as a sacred trust for the children of Michel, whose physical legacy was apparent in Jean-Louis's black eyes, the tiny birthmark close to Danièle's left ear, and Yves's drooping eyelid.

There were times when he could lull his feelings of remorse into unconsciousness, weeks together when he did not even think of it. But the need to conceal the manner of his life was something that never left him. His one hope was that he would die without the family ever suspecting him of concubinage. On this particular evening he was entirely without suspicion that Blanche was lying wide-eyed in the great pillared bed in which his brother had died, walled in by the airless Bordeaux darkness, thinking about him, and forcing herself to face the strangest of strange duties. Even at the risk of impoverishing her children, she must do all in her power to persuade her brother-in-law to get married. It wasn't enough merely not to dissuade him from regularizing the position. She must actively urge him to do what was right and proper. It was her duty to make this decision, whether or no it was heroic on her part to do so. . . . The very next day, she would force him into the open, would compel him to discuss this burning question, would open her offensive.

But he was far from being responsive to her suggestion. During dinner, Blanche took advantage of some casual remark let drop by Jean-Louis, to say something to the effect that there was still plenty of time for Uncle Xavier to settle down and have children of his own.

"I very much hope," she said, "that he has not given up the idea. . . ."

But he chose to treat the whole thing as a joke, into which he entered whole-heartedly, and proceeded with a certain nimbleness of humour which he could show on occasion, to describe the imaginary lady of his choice, much to the children's delight.

When they had gone to bed, and brother and sister-in-law were leaning together at the window, she made a valiant effort:

"You know, Xavier, I was quite serious in what I said at dinner. I should be quite honestly delighted to hear that you had decided to get married, no matter how late in the day."

His response to this was to say that he had no intention of ever getting married, and this he announced so drily that it was impossible for her to continue the discussion. There was

nothing in the incident to arouse his suspicions, for the idea of
making Joséfa his wife had never entered his mind. It would
be no less than sacrilege to give the Frontenac name to a woman
from nowhere, who had played fast and loose with her life.
To bring such an individual into his parents' house, to introduce
her to Michel's wife and Michel's children, was inconceivable.
Consequently it never occurred to him that Blanche might
have got wind of his secret. Irritated, but by no means worried,
he turned from the window, and asked whether she would
very much mind if he went to his room.

IV

SLOWLY the stream of childhood flowed, with that calm
regularity which seems to leave no room for chance or
accident. Every hour of every day was filled to the brim
with its appointed tasks and occupations – breakfast, followed
by school; the ride home in the bus; the stairs taken four at a
time; the smell of dinner; Mamma; *The Mysterious Island*;
bed-time. Even illness had its place (Yves's whooping-cough,
José's feverish cold, Danièle's scarlatina) in the ordered sequence
of events. It was a source more of pleasure than discomfort,
stressing a date, setting a landmark for memory – "the year you
had that attack of fever". . . A succession of summer holidays
opened into the pillared aisles of the Bourideys' pine-woods,
and the house now purged of Uncle Péloueyre. Were the noisy
cicadas the same as had scraped away a year before? From the
wine-growing estate at Respide came hampers of peaches and
greengages. Nothing changed except that Jean-Louis's and

José's trousers were lengthened. . . . Blanche Frontenac, once so slim, was developing a middle-aged spread, and beginning to worry about her health. She was convinced that she had got a cancer, and, tormented by this fear, worried incessantly about what would become of the children when she was no longer there. It was she, now, who took Yves in her arms, he who, at times, resisted. She had any number of medicines which had to be taken before and after meals, but never, for a moment, would she let anything interfere with her duty of bringing up Danièle and Marie in the way that they should go. The little girls already showed sturdy legs and large, sagging behinds. They were two little brood-mares in the making, and found an outlet for their maternal cravings in ministering to the children of various washerwomen and chars.

Easter, that year, fell so early that the Frontenac children were back at Bourideys by the end of March. Spring was in the air, though as yet the material signs of it were few. The oaks in their dress of last year's leaves seemed still constricted by the hand of death. From beyond the meadows the cuckoo called. Jean-Louis, his small-bore rifle on his shoulder, tramped the woods, fondly thinking he was out after squirrels, though really he was looking for the Spring. Spring prowled through the days of imitation Winter like someone whom one feels quite close but cannot see. Now and again he thought that he could smell it, only to find it gone again. It was cold. For one brief moment the afternoon light touched the trees with a soft finger, so that the pine-bark glowed like scales, its gummy wounds holding the gleam of sunset. Then, suddenly, everything went dull. The West wind drove the heavy clouds so low that they hung about the tree-tops, and drew from the ranks of sombre trunks a prolonged moaning. . . . It was as he approached the meadows watered by the Hure that Jean-Louis came at last upon the Spring caught in the river grasses which were already thick along the banks. It oozed from the sticky and half-opened alder buds. He leaned above the water to watch the living, floating tresses of the weed – the hair of those whose faces must, since the world's creation, have lain buried in the sand which had been worked into ridges by the river's gentle flow. The sun came out again. Jean-Louis leaned his back against an alder trunk, took from his pocket a school edition of the *Discourse on Method*, and for ten minutes paid no more attention to the Spring. Then his attention began to wander. His eyes lighted on the demolished hurdle which he had had put up in August as a jump for his mare "Tempest". He must tell Burthe to mend it. He would ride over tomorrow morning to Léojats . . . he would see Madeleine Cazavieilh. . . . The wind had moved into the east, and came to him rich with village smells – turpentine, warm bread, the smoke of wood-fires cooking humble meals. The mingled scent augured fine weather and filled the boy with happiness. . . . He began to walk through the grasses already drenched with moisture. Primroses were glowing on the sloping bank which closed the meadow to the west. The young man crossed it, skirted a recently cleared patch of heath, and made his way down the hill again towards the oak coppice through which the Hure flowed on its way to the mill. Suddenly he stopped dead, choking back a laugh. A queer little cowled monk was seated on a pine-root. He was holding a school exercise-book in his right hand, and was intoning to himself in a low voice. It was Yves, who had pulled the hood of his cape over his head, and was sitting there, stiff, still and mysterious, quite sure that he was alone, and behaving as though the angels had charge over him. Jean-Louis no longer wanted to laugh, because there is always something faintly terrifying in the sight of someone who believes himself to be unobserved. He felt shocked, as though he had broken in on a forbidden mystery. His first instinct was to move away and leave his younger brother to his incantations. But the love of teasing, all-powerful at that age, set him creeping towards the innocent object of his attention, whose sense of hearing was deadened by his hood. He hid behind an oak, a stone's throw from the root on which Yves sat enthroned, though too far from him to catch the sense of the words which escaped on the West wind. Then, with one bound, he was on top of his victim and, before the younger boy could so much as utter a cry, had snatched the exercise-book from his hand, and was racing at top speed for the park.

We never fully measure the effect of what we do to others. Jean-Louis would have been deeply distressed could he have seen the expression on the face of his younger brother, who stood there on the heath, as though turned to stone. . . . In a sudden access of despair, he flung himself to the ground, and lay with his face buried in the sand, muffling his cries. What, unknown to anyone, he had written, what was his, and his alone, what was a secret between himself and God, had been given now to others to mock and laugh at. . . . He began to run towards the mill. Was he, perhaps, thinking of the weir in which some years before a child had been found drowned? More likely, by far, that he had in mind, as often previously, to run just on and on, and never to go home again. But soon he was out of breath. His progress was slow because of the sand in his shoes, and because a pious child is ever borne up by angels. . . . "For he shall give his angels charge over thee: to keep thee in all thy ways. They shall bear thee in their hands: that thou hurt not thy foot against a stone. . . ." Suddenly a comforting thought came to him. Nobody in the world, not even Jean-Louis, could decipher his secret writing. It was more illegible even than the writing which he used at school. And

what *could* be made out would be unintelligible. It was idiotic
to work himself into a state. How could others possibly understand a language to which even he sometimes lacked a clue?

The sandy path ended at the bridge leading to the mill. The
meadows were hidden by the mist that rose from them. The
mill's old heart was still beating in the gathering dusk. A
horse's rough head was hanging over the half-door of the
stable. The low-built, humble, cottages with their smoking
chimneys, the stream, the meadows, all combined to make a
little clearing of greenery, of flowing water, and of hidden life,
framed within the ancient pine-trees of the parish. Yves had
his own ideas about them. At this hour the mystery of the
mill must not be disturbed. He retraced his steps. The first bell
began to sound for dinner. A shepherd's sharp cry rang through
the wood. He found himself caught in a rushing tide of dirty
wool, and his nose was assailed by a powerful stench of grease.
He could hear the lambs before he saw them. The shepherd
did not return his greeting, and his heart felt heavy. By the
great oak, which marked the beginning of the long ride, Jean-
Louis, holding the exercise-book in his hand, was on the look-
out for him. Yves stopped, a prey to uncertainty. Should he
be angry? A cuckoo uttered its last call over in the trees towards
Hurtinat. The two boys stood motionless, a few paces apart.
Jean-Louis was the first to move. He took a step forward:

"Not angry with me?"

Yves could never stand out against a kindly word, nor remain proof when a voice had more in it than usual friendliness.
Jean-Louis was frequently rough with him, was over-fond of
growling that he "needed a good shaking", and, what most
exasperated Yves, of saying – "when you get into the
army . . ." but this evening all that he remarked was:

"You aren't, are you?"

There seemed nothing to say. Yves put his arm about his

elder brother's shoulder. The latter freed himself from the embrace, but not unkindly.

"You know," he said, "they're most awfully good."

The other looked up, and asked him what was awfully good.

"What you've written . . . they're more than awfully good," he added with enthusiasm.

Together, they walked down the darkening ride between the pines.

"Are you laughing at me, Jean-Louis? – are you pulling my leg?"

They had not heard the second bell. Madame Frontenac came out on to the steps and cried:

"Children!"

"Look here, Yves, let's take a stroll in the park this evening, just the two of us. I want to talk to you: and – oh yes, bring the book."

In the course of the meal, José – who had bad table-manners, wolfed his food – as his mother never tired of telling him – and had not washed his hands, described his trip with Burthe into the heath-lands. The bailiff was training the boy to recognize the estate boundaries. . . . José's sole ambition was to become the "peasant" of the family, but he despaired of ever being able to pick up the boundary marks. Burthe would count the number of pines in a row, make his way through the furze, dig in the ground, and, lo and behold! a buried stone would come to light which had been set there by shepherd ancestors many centuries before. . . . These hidden evidences of tenure, concealed and overgrown, but always there, moved José to a sense of almost religious awe, which doubtless sprang from some hidden depth of race-memory. Yves, forgetful of his food, and glancing furtively at Jean-Louis, let his mind, too, dwell on these boundary marks of mystery. They came to life in his heart. They lay deep in that secret world brought by his poetry from the dark.

The two boys tried to leave the house without being seen. But their mother caught them. "The air's damp down by the stream. . . . Have you got your capes? . . . Whatever you do, keep on the move, and don't loiter."

The moon had not yet risen. The breath of winter was coming from the icy stream and from the meadows. At first they were at a loss to find the path, but very soon their eyes grew accustomed to the darkness. The upward thrust of the serried pines struck at the stars which hung above them, or seemingly, swam in the puddles of clear sky framed in the black tree-tops. . . . Yves, as he walked, felt that some weight had been lifted from him, that, deep within himself, a stone had been loosed by that elder brother who, from the distance of his seventeen years, was speaking to him in short embarrassed sentences. He didn't, he said, want to make Yves too self-conscious. He was afraid he might trouble the pool from which his inspiration flowed. . . . Yves reassured him, explaining that his poetry was first like hot lava which could not be controlled. Later, when the stuff had cooled, he worked on it, unhesitatingly scrapping adjectives, and removing all the odds and ends of rubbish which had been caught up in the molten mass. The young boy's certainty overcame all Jean-Louis' doubts. How old was Yves? Just turned fifteen . . . would genius outlive childhood?

"Which bits did you like best, Jean-Louis?"

It was an author's question: an author had just been born.

"It's so difficult to choose. I love the passage in which you describe the pines as absolving you from suffering, as bleeding in your stead, and of how you imagine them at night, weeping and growing weaker: the moaning is not theirs, you say, but the voice of the sea caught in their crowded tops. Oh, yes, and then that bit . . ."

"I know," said Yves – "the moon . . ."

They were without knowledge that on a March night in '67 or '68, Michel and Xavier Frontenac had been walking together along this same path. Xavier, too, had said "the moon" . . . and Michel had quoted the line – "*Elle monte, elle jette un long rayon dormant* . . ." Then, as now, the Hure was flowing on its silent way. After thirty years, the water was different, but not the sound of its rippling: and here, beneath the pines, was another love, and yet, the same.

"Mightn't it be a good thing to show them to somebody?" – Jean-Louis asked . . . "it did occur to me that perhaps the Abbé Paquignon" (his Professor of Rhetoric, whom he admired and respected) – "but I'm afraid that even he mightn't understand. He'd say that what you write isn't poetry, and, if it comes to that, it isn't. It's like nothing I've ever read. Criticism might worry you . . . might make you try to correct . . . anyhow, I must think about it."

Yves surrendered to a sense of complete confidence. The fact that Jean-Louis had testified to his productions was enough for him. He relied utterly on his big brother. All of a sudden, he felt ashamed, because they had been talking of nothing but his poems.

"And what about you, Jean-Louis? You aren't going to become a timber-merchant, are you? You won't let them do that to you? . . ."

"My mind's quite made up: the Normale, and a degree in philosophy . . . that's what I've got to do. . . . Isn't that mamma over there on the path?"

She had been afraid that Yves might catch cold, and had come out with a coat for him. When she reached them: "I'm growing heavy on my feet," she said, and leaned on her two sons . . . "are you sure you weren't coughing? Jean-Louis, didn't you hear him cough?"

The sound of their feet on the entrance-steps woke the girls, whose room looked out upon the terrace. The light in the billiard-room was dazzling, and they had to narrow their eyes.

Yves, as he undressed, looked at the moon over the motionless and brooding pines. No nightingale was singing as when his father, at the same age, had leaned from a window above the garden at Preignac. But the owl, perched on a dead branch, had, perhaps, a purer note.

V

NEXT day, Yves was not in the least surprised to find that his elder brother was, once again, his slightly churlish self, and behaved as though there were no secret between them. It was the scene of the previous evening that had seemed strange to him. It is enough for brothers to be aware that they are sprung from the same root, to know that they are twin suckers of the same plant. Such matters are not, as a rule, talked about between them. Of all loves, brotherly love is the least vocal.

On the last day of the holidays, Jean-Louis made Yves go out on "Tempest". As always happened, no sooner did the mare feel the boy's nervous knees against her flanks, than off she started at a gallop. Yves clung shamelessly to the saddle. Jean-Louis cut through the pines, and took up a position in the middle of the ride, with his arms outstretched. The mare pulled up short: Yves described a parabola, and found himself sitting on the sandy earth, while his brother announced that "he'd never be anything but a little sissy".

That was not what had shocked the younger boy. Something there was, however, that had come to him as a disappointment, though he did not like to admit it even to himself. The fact of the matter was that Jean-Louis was still paying frequent visits to the Cazavieilh cousins at Léojats. It was common knowledge to everyone in the family – and in the village, too – that each sandy track led, for Jean-Louis, to Léojats. In years gone by, the Cazavieilhs and the Frontenacs had fallen out over a will. But when Madame Cazavieilh died, they made up their differences though, as Blanche said, "there have never been any very warm feelings between us" . . . Nevertheless, on the first Thursday of each month she had got into the habit of asking Madeleine over. The girl already ranked as one of the seniors at the Sacred Heart, at a time when Danièle and Marie were still very low down in the school.

Madame Frontenac was conscious of two opposed feelings – anxiety on the one hand, pride on the other. She was always slightly uneasy when Burthe reported that "Monsieur Jean-Louis is a frequent visitor. . . ." She feared to see him tied up so young. At the same time, the knowledge that Madeleine would come into her mother's money when she married, was by no means unwelcome. Above all, she hoped that her great strapping son would be saved by a pure and passionate attachment from falling into evil ways.

Yves, for his part, was disappointed when, the day after that unforgettable evening, he learned in a few words exchanged with his brother that the latter had just come back from Léojats. Surely, what he had found in the school exercise-book should have turned his thoughts away from this lesser pleasure? Oughtn't everything, from now on, to seem, by comparison, trivial and colourless? To Yves, this love affair was merely a matter of languorous glances, snatched kisses, and much hold-

ing of hands – in fact, of all the romantic rubbish which he
held in such contempt. Now that Jean-Louis had penetrated
to his secret, had found his way into a world of marvels, what
was there for him to seek elsewhere?

No doubt Yves was already aware of the existence of young
girls. At High Mass at Bourideys, he admired the female
singers, with their long, white necks enhanced by black ribbons,
grouped round the harmonium, as on the edge of a shallow
bowl, and distending their throats which looked as though they
were already chock-full of maize and millet. His heart, too,
beat quicker when he saw the Dubuch girl – whose father was
the largest landlord of the neighbourhood – ride by on her
pony, the dark curls bumping on her skinny shoulders. Com-
pared to this sylph how gross did Madeleine Cazavieilh seem!
A great bow of ribbon bloomed on the hair which she wore
in a large coil on top of her head (a door-knocker, Yves called
it). She almost always sported a bolero, very short under the
arms, which accentuated the roundness of her buxom figure,
and a skirt which "flared" from a remarkably full waist-line.
When Madeleine Cazavieilh crossed her legs it was evident
that she had no ankles. . . . What charm could Jean-Louis find
in this lumpish young woman in whose placid face not a
muscle ever seemed to stir?

If the truth be told, Yves, his mother, and Burthe, would
have been not a little surprised could they have been present at
those visits: so little of any kind happened. It was as though
Jean-Louis had come to see, not Madeleine, but Auguste,
Cazavieilh. One great passion only did they have in common,
horses, and so long as the old man was with them, conversation
never flagged. But in the country there is never any peace and
quiet. Some farmer, or some local tradesman, is always sure
to want a word with the master. It is impossible to keep the
front-door shut as in a town. The two young people dreaded

the moment when Monsieur Cazavieilh would leave them alone together. Madeleine's calm exterior deceived all the world – except Jean-Louis. Perhaps what he loved in her more than anything else was a hidden surge of restlessness, invisible to others, which, as soon as they were left alone, broke through her seeming imperturbability.

On the occasion of Jean-Louis's last visit before the end of the Easter holidays, they walked together under the old leafless oaks which stood in front of the freshly plastered house, the walls of which bulged with age. Jean-Louis was talking about what he planned to do after he had left college. Madeleine was listening with close attention, as though his future concerned her no less than him.

"Naturally, I shall write a thesis . . . you can't see me remaining a simple schoolmaster all my life, can you? . . . I want to be a member of a university faculty."

She asked him how many months the thesis would take. He replied eagerly, that it wasn't a question of months, but of years. He spoke to her of the great philosophers. The essentials of their systems, he said, were already present in the theses they had offered. She, indifferent to the names he mentioned, dared not ask the one question which was of interest to her: would he put off marrying until he should have finished this work he spoke of? Was the preparation of a thesis compatible with family life?

"If I could get the job of a Reader at Bordeaux . . . but that is very difficult."

When she interrupted him with the rather foolish suggestion that her father might be able to pull strings, he protested acidly that he did not wish to be "indebted to a Government of Free-Masons and Jews". She bit her lip. As a daughter of a member of the General Council, a moderate Republican, who had no thought in his head but to be "on good terms" with everybody, she had been accustomed since childhood to see her father soliciting for all and sundry. There was not a decoration, not a job as road-surveyor or postman in the parish, which had not been given as the result of his good offices. She blamed herself for thus hurting Jean-Louis's feelings. Should the occasion arise, however, she would see what could be done, though she would be careful not to let him know what was in the wind.

Apart from these exchanges, some of which would seem to imply that their two lives might one day merge, the two young people made no gesture, nor exchanged a word, of tenderness. And yet, years afterwards, when Jean-Louis thought back to those morning visits at Léojats, his memory was of a happiness that had been not of this world. He saw, in the retrospect of imagination, little flurries of sunshine upon the crayfish stream and under the oaks. He followed Madeleine in recollection, and remembered how their legs had pushed aside the dense grasses, thick sown with buttercups and daisies in those old times of Whitsun holiday. They had walked upon the meadows as upon a sea. The winged beetles quivered in the light of the setting sun. No physical endearment could have added to their shared delight, might, indeed, have spoiled it, making a distorted image of their love. Not in words nor attitudes did the two young people give any formal shape to what held them breathless under the oaks of Léojats, to the immense and nameless wonder of their experience.

By what strange jealousy was Yves tormented! It was not caused by anything that Jean-Louis felt for Madeleine. His suffering came from the knowledge that another human creature could snatch his big brother from the life which they had always known, that the power to hold him in enchantment had passed from himself elsewhere. But these stirrings of pride did not prevent him from yielding to the humility of his years.

Jean-Louis in love meant for him Jean-Louis grown up. A youth of seventeen in love with a young girl, has no longer part or parcel in such things as happen in the world of those not yet of man's estate. For Yves, the poems he wrote belonged to the mysterious world of children's stories. Far from thinking of himself as "old for his age", he knew that the dream in which his work was born was that of childhood. Only if one was a child, he thought, could one share in so incomprehensible a game.

But when the day came for going back to Bordeaux, he realized how wrong he had been to lose confidence in his elder brother. . . . This revelation came to him at the moment least expected, and in the most unlikely place. At Langon station the Frontenac family had left the Bazas train, and were seeking, helplessly, for vacant seats in the express. Blanche was running down the platform. The children kept at her heels, dragging with them a basket containing a cat, birds in cages, a frog in a glass jar, several boxes of "souvenirs" – pine-cones, strips of tree-bark sticky with resin, and flints. With terror, the various members of the family were facing "separation". At that moment, the station-master approached Madame Frontenac, raised his hand to the peak of his cap, and told her that he was going to attach an extra second-class coach to the train. As a result of this, the Frontenacs found themselves all together in the same compartment, though bumped and shaken as one always is at the rear end of a line of railway coaches, breathless, but happy, and wondering audibly about the fate of the cat, the frog, and the umbrellas. It was just as they were drawing out of the station at Cadillac, that Jean-Louis asked Yves whether he had a "fair-copy" of his poems. Why, of course they had been copied into a handsome note-book, but Yves had not been able to change his hand-writing.

"Let me have them this evening, and I'll see what I can do. I may not be a genius, but my writing is extremely legible. . . . Why? . . . Can't you see, you little silly? But for heaven's sake, don't go getting ideas. . . . Our only chance is to get the professionals to grasp what you're after. We're going to send your poems to the *Mercure de France*. . . ."

Yves, pale to the lips, could only go on repeating that "that would be wonderful", Jean-Louis begged him again not to start counting his eggs before they were laid.

"They must get a whole pile of stuff every day. They probably chuck most of it into the waste-paper-basket unread. The great thing is to get someone to look at your stuff, someone who knows what's what. But you mustn't count on anything: it's one chance in a thousand – rather like throwing a bottle into the sea. Promise me that once the parcel's sent off you won't think any more about it?"

"Why, of course," said Yves: "no one'll ever look at them."

But his eyes were agleam with hope. He began to worry. Where could they find a big enough envelope? How many stamps would they have to put on it? Jean-Louis shrugged his shoulders. They would send the packet by registered post. He would look after all that part of the business.

At Beautiran a lot of people with baskets invaded the carriage. The Frontenacs had to crowd up together. Yves recognized one of his schoolmates, a country boy, a boarder, who was very good at games but with whom he had had nothing to do. They exchanged a brief greeting. Each was carefully studying the other's mother. Yves wondered what he would have thought of that fat, sweating woman if he had been her son.

VI

HAD Jean-Louis been at Yves's side during the swelter-
ing weeks which immediately preceded Prize-Day, he
would have put him on his guard against the folly of
waiting in daily expectation of an answer. But scarcely had
term begun than he took a decision which met with the admiring approval of all the members of the family, with the single
exception of his younger brother, to whom it was the cause
of profound irritation. Having made up his mind to take his
finals in Science as well as in Philosophy, Jean-Louis asked to
be allowed to become a temporary boarder, and so waste no
time in going to and from school. Yves made a point of addressing him as Mucius Scaevola. He had a horror, he said, of all
such manifestations of "nobility". Left to himself he had
thoughts for nothing but the fate of his manuscript. Every
evening, when the postman came, he asked his mother for the
key of the letter-box and rushed downstairs four steps at a
time. His hopes were regularly disappointed, but he consoled
himself with the thought that perhaps next day . . . He invented rational explanations for having to wait: manuscripts
would not, of course, be read as soon as they reached the office,
and then, no matter how enthusiastic the reader might be, he
would have to bring persuasion to bear on Monsieur Valette,
the editor of the *Mercure*. The blossoms on the chestnut trees
faded. The last of the flowering lilacs was alive with may-
bugs. The Frontenacs received from Respide so many hampers
of asparagus that they "didn't know what to do with it all".
Yves's hopes, like the water in the river-beds, fell lower with
every day that passed. He became embittered. The fact that his
nearest and dearest failed to detect a bright nimbus about his

head, made him hate them. They, for their part, and without intentional malice, were careful to sit on him. "If anyone squeezed your nose, milk would come out!" Yves was fully convinced that his mother was lost to him. He felt estranged from her by the things she said – pecks administered by the hen to the growing chick who would follow her about. If, he thought, he explained what he was feeling, she wouldn't understand. If he read his poems to her, she would merely treat him as a little silly, or as quite mad. He did not know that the poor woman had a far deeper knowledge of her youngest son than he could imagine. She knew perfectly well that he was different from the others, though in what way, precisely, she could not have said. He was the sole puppy of the litter with a touch of wildness.

It was not the others who despised him, but he himself who held firmly to the conviction that he was insignificant and worthless. His narrow shoulders and weak arms filled him with feelings of disgust. All the same, the ridiculous temptation came to him one evening, when the family was assembled in the drawing-room, to jump on the table and cry – "I am a king! I am a king!"

"It's just a phase . . . you'll see, it will pass" – that was Madame Arnaud-Miqueu's constant refrain, whenever Blanche unburdened herself. Yves never wore hats now, and washed his hands as seldom as possible. Since the *Mercure* remained silent, since Jean-Louis had abandoned him, since no one now would ever know that a remarkable poet had been born in Bordeaux, he would find food for his despair in making himself even more unpleasant to look at than he was; would hide his genius in a gaunt and grubby body.

He was seated one June morning in the school bus, reading over the most recent of his poems, when he noticed that his neighbour kept peering over his shoulder. . . . The boy in question was one of the seniors, a fellow called Binaud, who was in his philosophy year and a rival of Jean-Louis, than whom he seemed considerably older. . . . He had already started to shave, and his smooth, baby cheeks were covered with cuts. Yves pretended to have noticed nothing: but he moved his hand slightly so as not to impede the other's view, and was careful not to turn the page until he felt quite sure that the boy beside him had read to the bottom of the preceding one. Suddenly, the Nosy Parker, without a word of apology, asked him where he had "picked *that* up". Yves remained silent, and he pressed his question.

"Come on, tell me who wrote it?"

"Guess."

"Rimbaud? – no, of course not, you wouldn't know anything about him."

"Who's Rimbaud?"

"I'll tell you all about Rimbaud, if you'll tell me where you copied that poem."

Here, at last, was someone to take the place of Jean-Louis, the traitor. A stranger should be admitted to the secret of his glory and his genius. With flaming cheeks he said:

"I wrote it myself."

"No, really, joking apart?" Obviously, the other did not believe him. As soon as he was convinced that Yves was speaking the truth, he felt ashamed to think that he had been seriously interested in the outpourings of a mere kid. There couldn't be anything in it if *he* was the author. Somewhat lackadaisically, he said:

"You must show me some more of your stuff . . ."

Yves opened his brief-case, but the other checked him with a touch on the arm:

"Not now: I've got too much work to do. But if you happen

to be anywhere near the rue Saint-Genès on a Sunday evening, just ring the bell at 182 . . ."

Yves did not understand that he was being asked merely to leave his note-book there. To read his poems aloud to somebody! – what a dream of delight! Jean-Louis had never asked him to do that! In spite of his shyness, he could pluck up courage to read them to this stranger. The big fellow would listen with respect, and perhaps, as the reading progressed, with amazement.

Binaud was careful not to sit next to Yves again in the bus. But the younger boy found no reason for taking offence at that, because the examinations were approaching, and whenever the candidates had a moment, they buried their noses in their books.

He let two Sundays go by before making up his mind to call. With the dry heat of July, melancholy descended upon Bordeaux. No water trickled along the gutters. The cab-horses all wore straw hats with two holes in them for their ears. The new electric trams carried a cargo of collarless and shirt-sleeved men. The unbuttoned bodices of the women made them look hump-backed. Cyclists sweated at their task, their faces almost touching their handle-bars. Yves turned his head to see Madame Escarraguel's motor-car go by, making a noise like a wagon-load of old iron.

No. 182 rue Saint-Genès was a single-storeyed house of the kind that Yves knew as a "lean-to". He rang the bell. His mind was far away. No boy with the name of Binaud had any place in it. But the tinkling soon roused him. It was too late now to make his escape. He heard a door bang and the sound of a half-whispered confabulation. At last, a woman in a dressing-gown appeared on the threshold. She was thin, with a yellowish complexion. Suspicion gleamed in her eye. Her thick hair, of which she must have been very proud, seemed to have devoured her physical substance. It, alone, was living and luxuriant. The rest of her was wasted. Probably she was being eaten away by some internal tumour. Yves asked whether Jacques Binaud was in. The school cap in his hand must have reassured the woman, for she admitted him into the passage and opened a door in the right-hand wall.

It must once have been the drawing-room of the house, but was now transformed into a dressmaker's workshop. Paper patterns lay all over the table. An uncovered sewing-machine stood in front of the window. Obviously, the woman had been disturbed at her labours. A highly-coloured Salomé in terra-cotta, of Austrian manufacture, stood on the mantelpiece. Yves could hear somebody moving about next door, and the sound of an irritable voice – no doubt, Binaud's. . . . Without meaning to, he had intruded into the home of one of those "modest" state functionaries who are bitterly proud, for ever struggling to "keep up appearances", and careful to see to it that no stranger shall penetrate behind the scenes of their grinding lives. Obviously, Binaud had merely meant him to leave his manuscript, and nothing more . . . as was witnessed by the first words uttered by the youth when at last he appeared, coatless, and with his shirt unbuttoned. He had an enormous neck the back of which was a mass of small boils. So Yves had brought his poems, had he? He really shouldn't have gone to all that trouble.

"With the examinations only a fortnight off, I really haven't a moment, as you may imagine. . . ."

"You said . . . I thought . . ."

"I imagined you'd just drop your note-book in the next Sunday . . . but since you've come, let's have a look at 'em."

"No," said Yves; "no, I don't want to bore you. . . ."

He had only one wish, to get clear of this lean-to, this pervasive smell, this horrible youth. The latter, meanwhile, and no doubt on account of his friend, Jean-Louis, had recovered his temper and was trying to keep his visitor from going. But the boy had already made his way back to the street, and was now striding along in spite of the stuffiness, drunk with despair and resentment. . . . But he was only fifteen, and as soon as he reached the Cours de l'Intendance he went into Lammanon's tea-shop where he found consolation in an ice-cream. But when he left it, he found his sense of vexation waiting for him upon the pavement, a vexation out of all proportion to the visit which had gone so much awry. Every human being has his peculiar form of suffering, the laws of which take shape in earliest youth. So intense, on this particular evening, was Yves's wretchedness, that he felt he would never come to the end of it. He did not then know that he stood on the threshold of a whole sequence of glorious days, of weeks during which he would bask in the bright light of happiness, and that hope was about to bathe him in a radiance as changeless, and, alas, as deceptive, as the sunlight of the summer holidays.

VII

XAVIER FRONTENAC was now enjoying the most peaceful period of his life. His scruples had been set at rest, and since the capital sum promised to Joséfa had all been paid, there was no reason why he should not start putting money aside for his nephews. He was, on the other hand, still haunted by the dread that the family might get wind of her existence. His anxiety grew with the growth of the young Frontenacs, and gave him most trouble when they came within measurable distance of the age at which the risk of their being shocked, and even influenced by his sad example, was greatest. There was, however, comfort in the thought that once they were grown up they could begin to look after their property for themselves. He had made up his mind that, when he thought the right moment had come, he would sell his practice and go to live in Paris. He explained to Joséfa that the capital would provide them with a safe refuge. The earliest motor-cars were already making distances seem shorter, and he couldn't help but feel that Angoulême was very much nearer to Bordeaux than it had been in the old days. In Paris they would be able to go about together, and visit the theatres without risk of being recognized.

He had already taken steps to dispose of his practice. Although he would not actually give it up for another two years, he already had standing in his name a deposit account of considerably larger proportions than he had expected. So great was his satisfaction at this state of affairs that he felt justified in putting into effect a long-standing promise that he and Joséfa should make a circular tour of Switzerland. When he mentioned this she showed so little pleasure that he felt disappointed. The truth of the matter was that the prospect seemed so wonderful to the poor woman, that she could not really believe in it. Had it been merely a question of spending a week at Luchon, as they had done in '96, she could have taken it in . . . but to go to Paris, and on to Switzerland . . . well, she shrugged her shoulders and continued with her sewing. Nevertheless, when she saw Xavier deep in guides and time-tables, busily planning their itinerary, the incredible happiness did seem to be taking form and substance. She could no longer doubt that his mind was made up. One evening he appeared with the tickets actually in his pocket. Until that moment she had mentioned the trip to nobody, but now she decided that she could safely write to her married daughter at Niort. "I really don't know whether I am sleeping or waking. The tickets are safe and sound in the glass-fronted wardrobe. They have been taken in the names of Monsieur and Madame Xavier Frontenac. They are *family* tickets. I can hardly believe that it is true, my dear. The thought of them makes me come over all funny. *Monsieur and Madame Frontenac!* I asked him whether he would enter us like that in the hotel registers, and he replied that he could hardly do otherwise. My question put him in a bad temper – you know what he's like. . . . He said that he'd been three times to Switzerland and seen everything there except the mountains, because they had always been hidden in clouds, and it had rained all the time. I hadn't the courage to tell him that I shouldn't mind, because what'll please me most will be going to all those hotels as Xavier's wife, and only having to ring a bell for breakfast. . . ."

Monsieur and Madame Frontenac . . . These words, seen on the tickets, had not produced any great effect on Xavier, but, then, he had not foreseen that the problem of their identity would present itself afresh each time they arrived at an hotel. . . . Joséfa would have been much wiser not to have sown this new anxiety in his mind. It entirely spoiled his pleasure. What a fool he had been to pile up all this trouble for himself! – fatigue, expense, and the spectacle of Joséfa playing the great lady (to say nothing of the fact that the local papers would probably list them under the heading of "Visitors", as *Monsieur and Madame Frontenac*). But it was too late to start worrying now. The tickets were taken. The wine had been drawn.

On the afternoon of the second of August, the day before they were due to start, at the very moment when, in Angoulême, Joséfa was putting the finishing touches to an evening dress designed to dazzle the hotels of Switzerland, Madame Arnaud-Miqueu, walking along a street in Vichy, had one of those attacks of dizziness which she described by saying that her head felt as though "it was going round". This particular attack was sudden and violent. Her hand slipped from the arm of her Caussade daughter, and her head struck the pavement. She was carried back to the hotel, apparently at her last gasp. Next morning, at Bourideys, Blanche Frontenac was taking a last turn round the park before shutting herself away in the coolness of the house. It was already so hot that she found breathing difficult, and the cicadas one by one were breaking into a joyful cacophony. She saw Danièle running towards her, waving a telegram.

"Mother seriously ill. . . ."

Late that same afternoon, a telegraph boy knocked at Xavier Frontenac's door in Angoulême. Joséfa, who rarely ventured to visit him in his home, was, on this occasion, helping him with his packing, and had already, without a word to him, stowed away three of her own dresses in the trunk. As soon as she saw the slip of blue paper in Xavier's fingers, she knew they would not go.

"Oh, damnation . . . !"

The tone of Xavier's voice was, in spite of himself, almost cheerful, because, between the lines of Blanche's message – "Starting for Vichy mother seriously ill please come first train Bourideys look after children" – he could read the assurance that he would never have to write in the register of any Swiss hotel, the words – "*Monsieur and Madame Frontenac*", and that he would be fifteen hundred francs to the good. He passed the telegram across to Joséfa. She realized at once that her hopes were at an end. For fifteen years she had grown used to being sacrificed upon the altar of the Frontenac deity. As a mere matter of form, she said: "It's come too late: the tickets are taken: we have already started. Send a wire from the frontier that you are terribly sorry. . . . After all, the children are nearly grown-up" (from hearing them spoken about so often, she knew quite a lot) – "Monsieur Jean-Louis is close on eighteen, and Monsieur José . . ."

He interrupted her in a fury:

"What's come over you? Have you gone mad? Do you really think me capable of not responding when my sister-in-law appeals to me for help? . . . I've always told you that they must come first. . . . Cheer up, my dear, it only means putting off our holiday. We'll go another time. . . . Be sure to put on your cape, it's getting rather fresh."

With a docile gesture she resumed her dark brown cape with the braided frogs. The high, ruff-like collar framed, in the strangest way, her flabby face with that tip-tilted, "cheeky", nose which alone had the power to awaken memories of the past in him. She had a receding chin, and her hat, perched on top of a thick coil of yellow hair, was a tangle of convincing artificial convolvulus. It was easy to see that her hair, when "down", must reach to her waist. The weight of it broke all her combs. "Your hair's always a mass of pins!"

Submissive though she had become, the poor woman, as she fastened her cape, muttered something to the effect that "one of these days you'll find I've had just about as much as I can stand". Xavier told her sharply to repeat what she had just said, and this she did, though with no great air of conviction. Xavier Frontenac, who treated the members of his family with an excessive delicacy, who was almost morbidly scrupulous in his dealings with them, and in his handling of business matters, went out of his way to behave to Joséfa with a brutal lack of consideration.

"Now that you've made your little pile," he said, "you're at perfect liberty to clear out, if you want to. . . . But you're such a ninny that you'll lose every penny of it. . . . You'll be obliged to sell the furniture," he added, "unless – but don't forget that the bills are all in my name, as is the lease of the flat. . . ."

"What! isn't the furniture mine, then? . . ."

He had touched her on her most sensitive spot. She adored the big bed which had been bought at Leveilley's, in Bordeaux, with its gold fluting, and its head-board crowned by a torch and a quiver. Joséfa had long come to see the torch as a horn of plenty sprouting hair, and the quiver as a similar object filled with goose-feathers. . . . These strange symbols neither worried nor surprised her. The night-table, resembling a richly adorned reliquary, was far too beautiful, she always maintained, for what it held. But the pride and joy of her heart was the glass-fronted wardrobe. The ornamental pediment carried a design of the same horns of plenty interlaced by the same ribbons with an added motif of roses, so deeply carved and undercut that, according to Joséfa, one could count their petals. The mirror was set between two columns which were ribbed to half their height, and terminated, at their bottom end, in human torsos. The inside was of lighter wood which "showed up beautifully" the piles of drawers with lace borders "as broad as your hand", of underskirts trimmed with stiffly starched scallops, and of dainty camisoles – all of which were Joséfa's delight, such a passion did she have for "linen".

"What, isn't the furniture mine?"

She began to sob. He put his arms round her:

"Of course it's yours, you great baby."

"Actually," she said, wiping her eyes, "it's silly of me to cry, because I never really thought we should go. I thought there'd be an earthquake. . . ."

"Whereas, all that's happened is that old Madame Arnaud-Miqueu has taken it into her head to peg out."

He was in high good humour, overjoyed at the thought of joining his brother's children in the country.

"Poor Madame Michel will feel terribly lonely. . . ."

Joséfa thought endlessly, and with deep devotion, of the being whom she had grown accustomed to set on the highest of high eminences. There was a short silence, at the end of which Xavier said:

"If her mother dies, she will be very rich. There will no longer be any need for her to touch a penny of the Frontenac fortune."

He walked round the table, rubbing his hands.

"You must take the tickets back to the Agency. I'll drop them a line. They're clients of mine and won't make any difficulties. Keep the money they give you. . . . There's some of your allowance still owing, and it'll just about cover it" – he added gaily.

VIII

ON the day of Blanche's departure for Vichy (she was to take the three o'clock train), the family lunched in complete silence – that is to say, without speaking, for the absence of conversation made the noise of forks and dishes seem louder than it would have been otherwise. The children's appetite rather shocked Blanche. When she came to die, they would go on eating just as they were doing now . . . but, after all, hadn't she caught herself wondering, only a few moments ago, who would have the house in the rue de Cursol? Storm clouds had driven across the sun, and the shutters had had to be opened. The peaches were attracting the wasps. The dog barked, and Danièle said: "It's the postman." Every head was turned to the window, towards the man who had come from the warren, with his open box slung over his shoulder. Even in the most united of families there is always somebody who is waiting for, hoping for, a letter, of which the others know nothing. Madame Frontenac recognized the writing of her mother who might, at this very moment, be on her deathbed, or dead.... She must have written to her on the very morning of the accident. She hesitated to open the letter, finally made up her mind to do so, and burst into tears. The children were staggered at the sight of their mother's grief. She got up and left the room with her two daughters. No one, except Jean-Louis, had paid any attention to a large envelope which the servant had put in front of Yves. *Mercure de France* ... *Mercure de France*. Yves couldn't bring himself to open it.... Just a bit of printed matter ... that was all it was ... printed matter. His eye caught a sentence. It was about him: about his poems. ... They had got his name wrong: Yves Frontenoux. There was a letter. "Dear Sir, and dear Poet: in view of their unusual beauty, we have decided to print all the poems you have sent us. We should be obliged if you would correct the proofs and send them back by return of post. ... So high is our opinion of your work, that the idea of remuneration seems to us to be quite out of place. With every expression of admiration, I remain, dear sir and dear poet, yours sincerely, Paul Morisse. PS. I hope that, in the course of the next few months, I may be allowed to see some of your more recent productions. You will, however, understand that I cannot, in any way, commit this firm to any undertaking in the matter."

Three or four drops spattered the earth at long intervals, and then, at last, the rain set in, a quiet, persistent, downpour. Yves, in his deepest being, was conscious of its freshness. Like the leaves, he rejoiced in the rain. It was as though the clouds had burst on him, and on him alone. He passed the envelope across to Jean-Louis, who, after a quick glance, slipped it into his pocket. The younger children came back into the room. Their mother was calmer now, and would be down when it was time for her to start. . . . Grandmamma said in her letter – "the dizziness in my head is worse than ever. . . ." Yves made an effort to break from his happiness. It was round him like a fire: he could not escape the blaze. He forced himself to follow his mother's journey in imagination – three trains as far as Bordeaux, and then the Lyons express. She would change at Gannat. . . . He had no idea how to correct proofs . . . How could he send them back by return? . . . The letter had been forwarded from Bordeaux . . . that meant that a whole day had been lost already.

Blanche appeared, her face concealed by a falling veil. One of the children cried out – "Here's the carriage!" Burthe was having difficulty with the horse because of the flies. As a rule, the children squabbled about who should go with their mother in the victoria to the station, and come back, not on the letdown seats, but on the "springy cushions". But today, Jean-Louis and Yves ceded their right of precedence to José and the youngsters. They waved their hands and cried:

"We shall expect a telegram tomorrow morning."

At last! . . . there was no one now to dispute their sovereignty over house and park. The sun was shining through the raindrops. The wild weather had turned strangely mild. The wind in the water-logged branches produced an occasional short, sharp shower. The two boys could not sit down because the garden benches were soaked. Consequently, they read the proofs as they sauntered round the park with their heads close together. Yves said that now the poems were printed they seemed shorter. There were very few misprints, and such as there were they corrected by the artless method they would have used in revising a fair-copy in class. When they reached the great oak, Jean-Louis asked suddenly:

"Why haven't you let me see your latest poems?"

"You didn't ask me to."

Jean-Louis explained that he wouldn't have taken any pleasure in them while the examinations were looming. Yves offered to fetch them.

"Wait for me here."

He dashed away, running towards the house, drunk with happiness, his bare head thrown back. Deliberately, he plunged through the high clumps of broom and under the low-hanging branches, so as to feel the moisture on his face. The breeze created by his rapid progress seemed almost cold. Jean-Louis watched him bounding back towards him. This young brother of his, who looked so ill-kempt and squalid when in town, seemed almost to fly now with an angel's grace.

"Let me read them to you, Jean-Louis. I should so love to read them aloud. . . . Wait till I've recovered my breath."

They were standing with their backs to a tree and the younger boy could hear the beating of his fragile, over-driven heart against the ancient, living, trunk which always, when on the eve of departure at the end of the holidays, he would come to embrace. He began to read in an odd sort of sing-song which Jean-Louis at first thought silly, though, after the first few moments, he decided that no other tone would have been so suitable. Did he think these new poems less good than the earlier ones? He hesitated to pronounce: he would have to re-read them. . . . What bitterness, what sorrow, in one so young! Yves, who, just now, had bounded towards him like a fawn, was reading in a hard, harsh voice. And yet, his only feeling was one of profound happiness. He no longer felt anything of the appalling misery which these poems expressed. He was conscious only of the joy it gave him to have caught and fixed that misery in words which he felt to be eternal.

"You must send them to the *Mercure* at the beginning of the

October term" – said Jean-Louis. "There's no point in being in too much of a hurry."

"D'you like them better than the others?"

Jean-Louis hesitated:

"I think they go deeper."

As they approached the house they saw José and the younger children who had just got back from the station. They looked solemn and important. Marie said it had been awful to see mamma crying so when the train started. Yves turned away, afraid lest they might guess at his happiness. Jean-Louis hastened to find an excuse for him. After all, grandmamma wasn't dead yet. The news might have been exaggerated. This wasn't the first time she had received Extreme Unction – it had happened on three separate occasions . . . besides, Uncle Alfred had a weakness for making things out worse than they were.

Yves broke in thoughtlessly:

"He takes his hopes for fact."

"Oh, Yves, how can you!"

The children were shocked. But Yves was off again like a skittish foal, leaping the ditches, clutching to his heart the proofs which he was going to read for the third time in what he called his "house" – a place no better than a pig-sty, which stood in a wilderness of gorse. . . . There he would gnaw his bone to his heart's content.

José watched him running:

"What a nasty brat it is! – always glum when things are going well, and as happy as a dog with two tails when there's any bad news. . . ."

He whistled to Stop, and went off down the hill towards the Hure to set his ground lines, as unperturbed and happy as though his grandmother had not been at death's door. To feel drunk with happiness, his brother had needed but the first gleam of fame. It was enough for José to be a youth of seventeen with the summer holidays all before him, and a sure instinct for where the eels lay on the bed of the Hure.

IX

DINNER, in the absence of mamma, was noisier than usual. Only the girls, educated at the Sacred Heart, and trained to habits of scrupulosity, thought that "it was no time for joking". But even they could not help laughing when Yves and José imitated the singers round the harmonium in church, with their mouths all screwed up: *Rien pour me satisfaire dans ce vaste univers*. Jean-Louis, serious and sensible as ever, went out of his way to find excuses for himself and his brothers. If they laughed, he maintained, it was because of nervous excitement. Really and truly they felt just as sad as everybody else.

After dinner they went out into the dark night to meet Uncle Xavier who was due to arrive by the nine o'clock train. No matter how late they might be, the Bourideys train was always later still. Huge stacks of freshly-cut planks, exuding resin, stood in a circle round the station. The children wound their way between these obstacles, sustaining sundry bangs and knocks, and losing themselves in the tangle of sweet-scented alleys. Their feet sank deep into the carpet of trodden pine-bark. They could not see it in the darkness, but knew that by daylight it had the colour of dried blood. Yves maintained that the planks were no less than the broken limbs of pines. Torn and stripped, these sacred bodies of the martyrs scented the air.

"What a little ass!" growled José: "what's that got to do with it?"

They saw the gleam of the station lamp. A number of women were talking loud, and laughing. Their voices were piercing. There was something animal about them. The children went through the waiting-room and crossed the tracks. In the silence of the woods they could hear the distant sound of the little train, the rhythmic puffing which they knew so well, and often imitated in the winter days in Bordeaux, so as to remind themselves of the holidays. . . . There was a prolonged whistle, a sound of escaping steam, and the majestic toy emerged from the darkness. There was one traveller only in the second-class coach – it could be nobody but Uncle Xavier.

He had not expected to find them so cheerful. They fought over his bag: they clung to his arms: they went through his pockets till they found what sort of sweets he had brought them. He let them lead him like a blind man between the stacks of sawn planks, and breathed in, happy as always when he made this journey, the night smells of the ancient country of the Péloueyres.   He knew that at the road which skirted the town, they would exclaim – "Look out for Monsieur Dupart's dog!" When the last house had been passed, an opening would appear in the dark mass of the woods, a white streak which was the sandy path on which the children's feet would make their old familiar sound. Over there, in the distance, was the kitchen lamp, shining like a great star at ground level. . . . He knew that a delicious meal would be waiting for him, which the children, who had already dined, would not let him eat in peace. When he let some word drop about their poor grand-mother, he was greeted by a chorus of voices. They must wait for more accurate news. Aunt Caussade always exaggerated so. No sooner had he swallowed the last mouthful than he was dragged off to make the round of the park, in spite of the darkness. This was a rite which he was never allowed to omit.

"Smells good, doesn't it, Uncle Xavier?"

"It smells marshy," he replied quietly: "and I rather think I am going to catch a chill."

"Look at all the stars."

"I'd rather look where I'm walking."

One of the little girls asked him to recite *le méchant faucon et le gentil pigeon*. When they were small, he had amused them with old stories and bits of nonsense, to which they would always listen with undiminished pleasure and unvarying laughter.

"Aren't you ashamed at your age? – you're not children any longer, you know. . . ."

Again and again during the long days of happiness and sunshine, Uncle Xavier would say – "you're not children any longer . . ." but the miracle was precisely that they could still bathe in the waters of childhood even when childhood had long been passed. They were the beneficiaries of a marvellous respite, of a mysterious dispensation.

Next morning it was none other than Jean-Louis who said:

"Uncle Xavier, do make some fire-ships." He protested, for form's sake, but, that done, took a piece of pine-bark, shaped it into a ship with a few strokes of his knife, and set a lighted match upright in the hull. The current set the flame floating down the Hure, and the young Frontenacs felt again, as they had felt in days long ago, as they thought of the adventures lying ahead for this sliver of Bourideys pine-wood. The Hure would carry it as far as the Ciron; the Ciron flowed into the Garonne not far from Preignac . . . and at long last, the ocean would receive this little piece of wood from the park where all the Frontenacs had grown up. Not one of them would admit the possibility that it might get caught on a root, that it might rot into wreckage long before the Hure stream had carried it beyond the little town. It was essential, it was an act of faith, to believe that from this secret streamlet of Les Landes, the fire-ship would pass into the Atlantic Ocean, "with its cargo of Frontenac mystery" – as Yves put it.

These great boys ran along the bank as they had always done, to keep the fire-ship from going aground. The sun, already fierce, filled the cicadas with a drunken joy, and flies were swarming about every scrap of living flesh. Burthe brought a telegram, which the children opened with eager anxiety: "Slight improvement . . ." – How lovely! – they could enjoy themselves now, and laugh with a clear conscience. But in the days that followed there came a moment when Uncle Xavier, peering at the blue form, read out – "Grandmamma desperate . . .", and the children, in consternation, were hard put to it to know what to do with their happiness. Grandmamma Arnaud-Miqueu was dying in a hot bedroom at Vichy. But here, in the park, the long days of sunshine came to a blazing point. In the forest lands, no eye can see the storms gathering. For a long while they lie hidden behind the pine-trees. Only the rising wind betrays their presence. They leap upon the countryside like robbers from an ambush. Sometimes, copper-coloured clouds would swarm up from the south. A sighing in the branches would make the children say it must be raining somewhere.

But even on the days when the news from Vichy was bad, the silence and the brooding did not last for long. Danièle and Marie put their faith in a Novena which they were making for their grandmother in conjunction with the Carmelites of Bordeaux and the Convent of the Misericorde. José would announce that "something told him she would pull through". Uncle Xavier found it necessary to interrupt a Mendelssohn chorus which they were singing, in three parts, seated on the terrace.

Tout l'univers est plein de sa magnificence!
Qu'on l'adore, ce Dieu . . ."

"If only for the sake of the servants," he would say. But Yves protested that music was no bar to sadness and anxiety, and would wait until the glow of their uncle's cigar had vanished in the darkness of the garden path, to start up an aria from Gounod's *Cinq-Mars*, in his funny, breaking voice.

Nuit resplendissante et silencieuse

He addressed himself to the night as he might have done to a person whose fresh, warm touch he could feel, whose breath was upon his face:

Dans tes profondeurs, nuit délicieuse

Jean-Louis and José, seated on a bench at the top of the steps, leaned their heads back and looked at the shooting-stars. The girls cried out that a bat had got into their room.

At midnight, Yves re-lit his candle, having armed himself with the note-book which he used for his poems, and a pencil. Already the town cocks were replying to their brothers in the remote, forgotten farmsteads. Bare-footed, and in his shirt-sleeves, he leaned at his window and watched the sleeping trees. No one but his Guardian Angel would ever know how closely he resembled his father at the same age.

One morning, a telegram bringing the message "No change", was interpreted as being reassuring. The day was glorious. Distant storms had yielded a touch of coolness. The girls took alder twigs to their uncle for him to cut into whistles. But they insisted that no detail of the operation, none of the sacred rites, should be omitted. In order to strip the bark it was not enough that he should tap the wood with the handle of his penknife. He had also to sing a song in patois:

> *Sabe, sabe caloumet. Te pourterey un pan naouet.*
> *Te pourterey une mitche toute caoute, Sabarin,*
> *Sabaro . . .*

The children took up the idiotic and sacrosanct words in chorus. Uncle Xavier broke off in the middle of what he was doing:

"Aren't you ashamed, at your age, to make me play the fool like this?"

But all of them felt obscurely that, as the result of some singular favour shown by the gods, Time had stood still. Power had been given them to leave the train which nothing halts. In the very process of growing up, they could stand in the shallows of childhood, could dawdle while childhood slipped away for ever.

★   ★   ★

The news about Madame Arnaud-Miqueu improved. Things were going better than could have been hoped. Very soon now mamma would be back, and with her there they would have to curb their irresponsible foolishness. The special brand of Frontenac laughter would have to cease.

They set off to meet her. She, too, was coming by the nine o'clock train. There was a moon. The light filtered between the stacks of sawn planks. There had been no need to bring a lantern.

On their return from the station, the children watched their mother as she ate. She had changed. She looked thinner. She described how, one night, grandmamma had been so ill that a winding-sheet had been got ready (when guests die in large hotels, their bodies are removed at once, under cover of darkness). She noticed that they were scarcely listening, that there was some sort of understanding between the children and their uncle, made up of private jokes and words with special meanings. She felt as though she were confronted by a world of mystery into which she had not the right of entry. She stopped talking and relapsed into a mood of gloom. She had not against her brother-in-law the same grounds of complaint as once she had had, because now that she was older the nature of her demands on him was different. But the children's special brand of affection for him wounded her. She hated the knowledge that all their gratitude should be for him.

Blanche's return broke the charm. The children were children no longer. Jean-Louis spent all his time over at Léojats, and Yves began to suffer again from pimples. . . . He had slipped back into his moody and mistrustful attitude. The arrival of the *Mercure* with his poems included in the table of contents did nothing to take the scowl from his face. At first he lacked the courage to show them to his mother or to Uncle Xavier, and when, at last, he brought himself to do so, his worst fears were realized. His uncle could make nothing of them, and quoted Boileau: "What is truly conceived must be clearly expressed." His mother could not help having a momentary feeling of pride, but concealed it. She begged Yves not to leave the Review lying about, because it contained a " disgusting contribution" by a "certain Rémy de Gourmont". José, spluttering with laughter, read out the passages which he found most completely "loony". Yves rushed at him in a fury, and got a good licking for his pains. He found consolation in the many letters he began to receive from unknown admirers. From now on, these continued to arrive, though he failed to realize to the full the significance of that fact. The orderly Jean-Louis found genuine delight in filing and indexing these evidences of success.

In the first storm-laden days of September, the Frontenacs began to get on each other's nerves. They lost their tempers. Quarrels flared up for no particular reason. Yves would throw down his napkin and leave the table; Madame Frontenac would go to her room, and when she came down again, after repeated embassies and deputations of remorseful children, her eyes were often swollen and her face puffy.

X

THE storm of which these were the premonitory rumb-lings, broke on the September Feast of Our Lady. After luncheon, Madame Frontenac, Uncle Xavier, and Jean-Louis were closeted together in the small drawing-room. The double doors were open, and in the billiard-room beyond, Yves was lying down, trying to get some sleep. The flies were plaguing him, and a large imprisoned dragonfly was bumping against the ceiling. In spite of the heat, the two girls were careering round the house on bicycles, each in a different direc-tion, and uttering screams of delight every time they passed one another.

"We must fix the date of the luncheon before Uncle Xavier leaves," Madame Frontenac was saying. "You must make the necessary arrangements with nice Monsieur Dussol, Jean-Louis. You're going to have to spend most of your life with him, you know, and . . ."

Yves was delighted to hear Jean-Louis's vehement protest:

"No, mamma . . . I keep on telling you, but you won't listen. I have no intention of going into the business."

"That is mere childishness on your part. I refuse to pay any attention to it. . . . You know perfectly well that, sooner or later, you will have to make up your mind to take your rightful position in the firm – and the sooner, the better."

"Dussol may be an excellent fellow," put in Uncle Xavier, "and deserving of the fullest confidence. But the fact remains that it is high time – and more than high time – that a Frontenac was in charge."

Yves had half risen, and was straining his ears.

"I'm not interested in the business."

"What, may I ask, are you interested in?"

Jean-Louis hesitated for a second, went very red, and then boldly announced:

"Philosophy."

"Are you completely out of your mind? Philosophy indeed! You'll do exactly as your father did before you, and your grandfather before him. Philosophy is not a profession!"

"As soon as I've got my degree, I intend to start work on my thesis. I shall take my time over it . . . and eventually I shall get a university post. . . ."

"So that's your ideal, is it!" exclaimed Blanche: "to be a state employee – did you hear that, Xavier? – a state employee! – a young man with the finest business in Bordeaux waiting for him to step into!"

It was at this point that Yves entered the room. His hair was tousled, his eyes blazing. He advanced through the cloud of smoke with which Uncle Xavier's everlasting cigarette enveloped faces and furniture.

"How can you compare . . ." – he began in a shrill voice – "how can you compare the trade of a timber-merchant with the vocation of a man who has dedicated his life to the things of the spirit? . . . it's . . . it's indecent!"

The two elders were dumbfounded. They stared at the

young enthusiast standing there before them in his shirt-sleeves, and with his hair falling over his eyes. His uncle told him in a trembling voice to mind his own business. His mother ordered him to leave the room. But, without paying the slightest attention to them, he went on with his tirade. It was only to be expected, he said, that in such a completely unmeaning place as Bordeaux, a merchant of any kind should rank higher than a scholar, that a wholesale wine-dealer should regard himself as of more importance than a man like Professor Pierre Duheim of the Science Faculty, whose name would probably be entirely unknown there, if it wasn't that people thought he might be useful at cramming brainless young fools for their Finals! (Yves would have felt not a little embarrassed if he had been asked to give a concise account of Professor Duheim's labours.)

"Listen to him standing up and speechifying! . . . You're nothing but an unlicked cub, my boy. Why, if anybody squeezed your nose . . ."

Yves completely ignored the interruption. It wasn't, he said, only in this idiotic town that the things of the mind were held in contempt. All over the country teachers and intellectuals were starved and neglected. . . . "In France their name is mud: in Germany, the word professor is equivalent to a title of nobility. . . . But, then, the Germans are a great people! . . ." He continued, his voice getting shriller and shriller, inveighing against all patriotism and all patriots. Jean-Louis tried in vain to stop him. Uncle Xavier, now quite beside himself, was going on and on without producing the slightest effect:

"*I've* nothing to be ashamed of . . . everyone knows which side *I'm* on. . . . From the very beginning I believed in Dreyfus's innocence . . . but I won't let a young cub like this . . ."

It was then that Yves allowed himself to indulge in a reference to the "defeated of '70" – a piece of insolence so crude that it served to steady him. Blanche Frontenac had risen to her feet:

"So now you insult your own uncle! . . . Leave the room at once, and don't let me see you again!"

He crossed the billiard-room and went down the steps. The blazing heat opened before him and closed again behind. He plunged into the stifling airlessness of the park. Clouds of flies hung buzzing close above the ground. Horseflies clung to his shirt. What he was feeling was not so much remorse as humiliation. He was ashamed at having lost his head and struck out blindly. He should have remained calm and stuck to the point at issue. They were right . . . he was just a kid. . . . It had been horrible of him to say that to his uncle, unforgiveable. How could he get back into favour? The odd thing was that both his mother and his uncle had emerged from the quarrel quite undiminished in his eyes. Though he was still too young to put himself in their shoes, and to understand their point of view, he passed no judgment on them. Mamma and Uncle Xavier were still, as they had always been, special and privileged beings. They formed part of his childhood, were elements in a romantic whole from which it was not in their power to isolate themselves. No matter what they might do, no matter what they might say, thought Yves, they remained inseparable from the mysterious climate of his own existence. They might blaspheme against the things of the spirit, but it made no difference. The spirit dwelt in them, and, though they did not know it, shed a radiance about their feet.

Yves turned back. A threat of storm had dulled the sky. But as yet there was no rumbling of thunder. The cicadas had fallen silent, but there was an intense quivering in the air above the meadow grasses. He walked on, shaking his head like a young colt in an effort to free himself from the horse-flies, which made no effort to escape but let themselves be crushed when he slapped at face and neck. . . . "One of the defeated of '70" . . . He had not meant to be offensive. The children made a regular practice of pulling Uncle Xavier's leg about the way in which he and Burthe had enlisted as volunteers, and how they had never so much as clapped eyes on a Prussian. But this time the words had contained something more than a joke.

He went slowly up the steps and came to a halt in the vestibule. The others were still in the small drawing-room. Uncle Xavier was holding forth: " . . . the day before I was due to go back to the regiment I decided to pay one last visit to my brother Michel. I jumped over the wall of the barrack-yard and broke my leg. In hospital I was put in a ward with the smallpox patients. I might have died there. . . . Your poor father, who knew nobody in Limoges, made so many representations that he finally succeeded in getting me out. Poor Michel, he had tried so hard to join the army, but it was no good (it was the year he went down with pleurisy). . . . For months and months he hung on in that appalling town, where he could see me only for one hour each day. . . ."

He stopped suddenly. Yves had appeared on the threshold. He saw his mother's glowering face turned towards him, and Jean-Louis's anxious eyes. Uncle Xavier did not so much as glance at him. He could not think of anything to say. But at heart he was still only a child, and it was the child who came to his rescue. Without a word he flung his arms round his uncle's neck, and kissed him. The tears were pouring down his cheeks. Then he went to his mother and perched himself on her knee, burying his face in her shoulder as he had been accustomed to do when he was very young.

"It's all very well being sorry, but my boy must learn to control himself, and not give way to temper . . ."

Jean-Louis got up and crossed to the window. There were

tears in his eyes. He held out his hand and announced that he had felt a drop of rain. . . . Nothing that had happened could be of the least use to *him*. The rain was closing in on them – a great spider's web, a net imprisoning him in this small and smoke-filled room. He would never escape from it – never.

It had stopped raining. Jean-Louis and Yves were walking along the ride that led to the great oak.

"You're not going to give in, are you, Jean-Louis?"

The other made no answer. His hands were in his pockets, and his eyes were on the ground. He was kicking a pine-cone before him. But his brother would not leave the subject. At last he spoke in a voice which lacked conviction:

"They tell me it's a duty to all of you: that, left to himself, José wouldn't amount to anything in the business. Once I'm in control, he can be taken in. . . . They even seem to believe that the day will come when you, too, will be only too glad to join me. . . . Now, don't go off the deep end. They can't, you see, understand the kind of person you are. Would you believe it, they've even foreseen the possibility that Danièle and Marie might get hooked up with chaps who've got no regular jobs. . . ."

"No one could accuse them of not looking ahead!" – exclaimed Yves (it made him furious to think that they actually believed it possible that he, too, might one day settle down to the family feeding-trough) – "Oh, they don't leave anything to chance! They organize everybody's happiness. They can't understand that one might prefer to be happy in one's own way! . . ."

"To them," said Jean-Louis, "it isn't a question of happiness but of acting for the common good, and in the interests of the family. . . . No, it's not a question of happiness. . . . Have you noticed how they never use the word? . . . Happiness . . . I've never seen mamma without that worried and tormented look on her face. . . . If Papa had lived, I don't think it would have made any difference. . . . No, not happiness but duty . . . a certain form of duty which they never shirk . . . and the awful thing, old man, is that – I understand their point of view!"

They had managed to reach the great oak before the rain started again. They could hear the shower pattering on the leaves. But the living bulk of the tree sheltered them beneath its mass of foliage which was thicker than any growth of feathers. Yves, a shade bombastically, spoke of the only real duty, the duty to what we carry within us, to our work – to a Secret word of God, which must be communicated . . . the Message with which we have been entrusted.

"Why d'you say 'we' – speak for yourself, Yves. I believe that you *are* someone with a message, that you *do* carry a secret within you. . . . But how should our mother and our uncle know it? So far as I am concerned, I have a horrid feeling that they may be right. As a teacher I should do no more than explain what other men have thought . . . though even that is one of the finest things in all the world to do . . . work that's enormously worth while giving one's life to. . . ."

Stop jumped out of a bush and dashed towards them with his tongue hanging out. José could not be far off. Yves addressed the muddy dog as though it had been a human.

"Been down in the marsh, haven't you, old man?"

A moment later, José, too, emerged from the underbrush. With a laugh, he displayed his empty shooting-bag. He'd been flogging the Téchoueyre marshes all morning.

"Not a thing! . . . a few landrail, but all of them out of range . . . I dropped a brace of moorhen, but couldn't retrieve 'em. . . ."

He had not shaved that morning. A young stubble showed dark on his childlike cheeks.

"I'm told there's a wild boar out Biourge way."

By nightfall the rain had stopped. For a long while after dinner, under a late moon, Yves watched Jean-Louis pacing up and down between his mother and his uncle. He saw the three shadowy forms turn into the gravel path. Then, the dark patch made by their figures emerged from the pine-trees into the moonlight. Blanche's vibrant tones dominated the talk, interrupted, from time to time, by Xavier's thinner, sharper, tones. Jean-Louis was silent. Yves had a feeling that his brother was lost, that he had been caught in a trap, that there was no hope of his freeing himself. . . . "They shan't get *me* . . ." But even while he was working himself up into a state of resentment against his family, he knew in some obscure fashion that, of them all, he alone clung desperately to his childhood. The King of the alders should never lure him to his unknown realm . . . unknown? . . . Ah, known only too well! The alders from which came that voice of terrible sweetness, are called by dwellers in a Frontenac country, "vergnes", and droop their loving branches above a stream the name of which is part of their secret knowledge. The King of the alders had stolen no Frontenac children from their cradles. What he had done was to prevent them finding a way of escape from childhood. He wrapped them in the winding-sheets of their dead lives, burying them beneath a weight of lovely memories and rotting leaves.

"I am going to leave you alone with your uncle" – Blanche said to Jean-Louis.

She passed close to Yves without seeing him. But he saw her. The moon shone full on her tortured face. Thinking herself alone, she had slipped her hand beneath her blouse. That gland was worrying her . . . all very well to keep on assuring her that it was nothing. . . . She felt it with her fingers. She must not die before Jean-Louis had taken his place as the head of the family business, as the master of the family fortune, as the younger ones' protector. She prayed for her brood. Her eyes, gazing upwards at the sky, saw Our Lady of Perpetual Succour, whose lamp in the cathedral she maintained, spread her enveloping cloak about the Frontenac young.

"Listen to me, my boy" – Uncle Xavier was saying to Jean-Louis. "I am going to talk to you as I would to a man. I have failed in my duty to all you children. I should have taken the place left vacant in the business after your father's death. . . . It is for you to make up for my shortcomings. . . . No, don't protest . . . You are about to say, aren't you? that I was under no compulsion. But you've got enough of the family feeling to realize that I deserted my post. It is for you to join up the ends of the chain which I broke. There is nothing tedious, I assure you, in running a great business which, perhaps, will provide shelter for your brothers, for your sisters' husbands, and, later, for your children. . . . By degrees we can buy out Dussol. . . . All this doesn't mean that you won't be able to keep abreast of what is going on in the world. . . . Your education will be an asset. . . . I was reading, only the other day, an article in the *Temps* which set out to show that knowledge of Greek and Latin and the Humanities is a fine training for future captains of industry. . . ."

Jean-Louis was not listening. He knew that he was beaten. Inevitably, in the long run, he would have surrendered. He was fully aware of the argument which carried most weight with him. Only just now, his mother had said: "We'll have Dussol, and I see no reason why we shouldn't invite the Cazavieilhs too . . ." A moment later she had added: "Once your military service is over, there'll be nothing to stand in the way of your getting married, if you want to."

It was Uncle Xavier now who was walking beside him in a scented cloud of cigar smoke. But an evening would come when it would be a young and rather stocky woman. . . . He could anticipate his calling-up date, and so be free to marry when he was twenty-one. Two more years, and then, all due formalities accomplished, he would be making the round of the park at Bourideys in the darkness, with Madeleine. All of a sudden the thought of marriage and its delights set him trembling from head to foot. His breath came short and sharp. He could smell the wind which had touched the oaks of Léojats in passing, had swept, in the moonlight, round the white house, and filled with its whispering the cretonne curtains of the room where Madeleine was lying, perhaps unable to sleep.

XI

"IT'S a Fouillaron . . . came from Bordeaux in three hours . . . seventy kilometres . . . not a hint of trouble the whole way. . . ."

Madame Frontenac's guests were crowded round Arthur Dussol, who was still buttoned up to the neck in his grey, dust-proof coat. He took off his goggles, and smiled, screwing up his eyes. Cazavieilh, who was bending over the car, with a mingled expression on his face of respect and mistrust, was trying to think of some question to put to its owner.

"Adjustable transmission-belt, you see," said Dussol.

"I needn't ask whether it's the latest model," remarked Cazavieilh.

"Brand new. No one can say" (and Dussol gave the flicker of a smile) "that I'm ever behind the times."

"True enough: one's only got to take a look at your mobile sawing-plant to see that. . . . What, if I may ask, are the special features of this car?"

"Only a short while ago" – began Dussol, as though lecturing to a class – "the normal form of transmission was by chains. But that's a thing of the past. . . . It's all done now by means of adjustable belts."

"What an A1 notion," said Cazavieilh. "Just two adjustable belts – eh? – is that all?"

"Synchronized, of course – it's the chain-belt system. Think of it this way: two cones working quite independently . . ."

Madeleine Cazavieilh led Jean-Louis away. José, who was passionately interested in this talk of cars, questioned Monsieur Dussol on the subject of gears.

"One can vary the speed as much as one likes by means of a simple lever" (Monsieur Dussol, with his head thrown back, and a look of almost religious gravity, seemed prepared to lift the habitable globe) – "just as in the steam-engine," he added.

Dussol and Cazavieilh sauntered slowly off. Yves followed them with his eyes, fascinated by their air of importance, by the self-satisfaction which seemed to drip from them. Now and again they came to a halt in front of one of the pines, looked it up and down, argued about its probable height, and tried to guess its girth.

"What should you put it at, Cazavieilh? . . ."

Cazavieilh mentioned a figure. Dussol gave a great laugh, so that his stomach, which looked as though it were an extra protuberance fastened on to his body, shook.

"You're a long way out!"

He took a measuring tape from his pocket, put it round the trunk, and said with an air of triumph:

"See? – I wasn't so far off, was I?"

"How much d'you think one could get from a tree this size, in terms of planks?"

Dussol brooded over the pine in meditative silence, while Cazavieilh, also silent, watched him in an attitude of respect, waiting for the verdict. Dussol took out his note-book, and plunged into a series of calculations. At last he gave his opinion.

"I'd never have believed it!" said Cazavieilh. "Wonderful, that's what it is, wonderful!"

"I find my eye comes in very useful at sales!"

Yves went back towards the house. The fine September morning was rich with an unaccustomed fragrance of truffles and sauces. He wandered round to the kitchens. The hired butler was in a bad temper, because they had forgotten to decant one of the wines. Yves went through the dining-room. The Dubuch girl would be between him and José. He re-read the Menu: *lièvre à la Villafranca, passage de mûriers*, then left the house again and went into the stable-yard where Dussol, a folding-rule in his hand, was measuring the distance between the wheels of a tilbury.

"What did I tell you? – out of the straight: this tilbury of yours wants a lot doing to it: if you don't believe me, measure it up for yourself."

It was Cazavieilh's turn now to squat down beside Dussol. Yves gazed in amazement at the spectacle of the two enormous rumps. At last the two men scrambled to their feet, scarlet in the face.

"You're absolutely right, 'pon my word you really are extraordinary, Dussol!"

A silent chuckle set Dussol quivering. He was bursting with conceit. His eyes were almost invisible. He had just enough intelligence to calculate the profit to be made out of people and objects.

He and Cazavieilh went back towards the house. Now and again they would both of them come to a full stop, gaze at one another as though engaged in resolving some problem concerned with the eternal verities, and then, start off again. Yves, motionless in the middle of the path, felt himself swept suddenly by an intoxicating, a horrible, craving to draw a gun and let fly at them treacherously, from behind: Bang! – right in the back of the neck! Over they'd roll: bang! – bang! – why wasn't he an Emperor, a negro despot!

"I'm a monster!" – was what he said aloud.

The hired butler appeared at the top of the steps:

"Luncheon is served!"

" . . . With the fingers, of course! . . ."

They began to wolf the crayfish, cracking the shells and sucking out the contents with an air of absorbed attention, as though they were torn between a desire to leave nothing in the dish, and a concern to observe the dictates of good manners.

Yves observed at close range the brown-skinned, fragile arm of the Dubuch girl; a child's arm attached to a shoulder which, for all its roundness, produced somehow the impression that it was immaterial. He lacked the courage to do more than shoot a sidelong glance at her face. The eyes were too large: the wings of the nose were wings indeed. The mouth alone, which was fleshy to excess and lacking in colour, struck a human note in this angelic physiognomy. The general view was that it was a pity she had so little hair, but her method of doing it (with a central parting and two coils over the ears) revealed a type of beauty which the world at large has only gradually come to appreciate – the contour of an exquisitely moulded head, the pure lines of a nape. Yves was reminded of the repro-

ductions of certain Egyptian bas-reliefs in a book on Ancient
History which he had used at school. Such pleasure did he find
in merely looking at this young girl that he made no attempt
to talk to her. At the beginning of the meal he had said that
living in the country must give her plenty of time for reading.
To this observation she had barely deigned to reply, and was
now deep in talk with José about riding and shooting. Yves
had been accustomed to seeing his brother dishevelled and
badly-dressed – a "real man of the woods", as he had called
him, and was surprised to notice that today for the first time, his
hair was smarmed down, his sun-tanned cheeks closely shaved,
and his teeth a glittering white. But the most remarkable thing
of all was that he was talking. José who, in the family circle,
never uttered a word, was actually making his neighbour
laugh! She was quite obviously infatuated: – "How silly you
are! I suppose you think that funny!" José never took his eyes
off her. There was a fixed look on his face which Yves was
too inexperienced to recognize as the very mark and signal of
desire. He remembered, however, what their mother had so
often said: "– José's the one who is going to need watching. . . . I shall have my work cut out with him. . . ." He never
missed a village fair or fête. Yves thought it stupid of him to
find so much pleasure in lucky-dips and merry-go-rounds. But
on the most recent of these occasions, he had discovered that
his brother had given a miss to the wooden horses, and had
spent his time dancing with the farmers' daughters.

All of a sudden, he felt sad. It was ridiculous to suppose that
the Dubuch girl, who was seventeen, could really take José
seriously. All the same, she was enjoying his jokes. There was
an understanding between them which went deeper than
words. It had nothing in it of deliberate intention, but was
controlled by the pulsing of their blood. It occurred to Yves
that he was jealous, and he felt ashamed. The real truth was

that he was conscious of being ignored, isolated. He did not say to himself – 'I, too, one of these days, and perhaps quite soon . . .'

At the other end of the table, Jean-Louis and Madeleine Cazavieilh were looking precisely as they were to look on the occasion of their betrothal. . . . Yves, who was drinking all the different wines which accompanied the meal, glanced down the table, along the avenue of faces, to where, at the far end, he could see in a haze that elder brother who had fallen into the pit from which he would never succeed in escaping. Beside him, the lovely female who had served as bait, sat quiet, relaxed and happy, her task accomplished. She was not, really, so stocky a figure as she appeared to Yves. She had given up wearing boleros, and had on a white muslin dress which left her handsome arms, and the pure line of her neck, exposed. Her appearance was at once ripe and virginal. She was waiting. Occasionally, she and Jean-Louis exchanged a few words. Yves wished that he could hear what they were saying. Had he done so, he would have been amazed to find how vapid were their interchanges. 'We' – Jean-Louis was thinking – 'have all our lives before us: time enough in which to get to know one another. . . .' They were discussing the mulberries which had just been put before them, and had been so difficult to get hold of, pigeon-shooting, the setting of decoys which would have to be done soon, because the wood-pigeons which herald the coming of the wilder species, would soon be here. . . . All the space of their two lives in which to explain to Madeleine . . . explain what? It was hidden from Jean-Louis that, as those years sped by, existence, for him, would be beset with many dramas, that he would have children, and lose two of them, that he would make an enormous fortune which, towards the end of his life, would collapse – and that through all the changes and chances husband and wife would continue to talk about the same simple, silly things which had been all-sufficient for mutual happiness in this dawning moment of their love, as they sat through an interminable meal, while the wasps buzzed round the piles of fruit, and the ice-pudding melted into a pinkish cream.

Yves contemplated this trivial happiness of Jean-Louis and Madeleine with feelings that partook at once of envy and con tempt. Not once had the Dubuch girl turned towards him. José, the great eater of the family, quite forgot to give himself a second helping of the different dishes. But, like Yves, he was indulging freely in the wines. A light dew of sweat was beading his forehead. Such was the power of the girl's eyes that, when she let them dwell for a moment on some man in whom she took not the slightest interest, he at once imagined that their glorious radiance had been kindled for him alone. The be-witched José decided in the secrecy of his heart that before the night was much older he would take the young enchantress for a stroll.

"You won't go without paying a visit to my pigeon-farm, now, will you? – promise!"

"What, over at Maryan? You must be cuckoo! It's a good half-hour's walk!"

"We could talk there undisturbed."

"Oh, I've had quite enough of your talking, thank you . . . just a lot of nonsense!"

Suddenly, she turned to Yves: her eyes were shining.

"How terribly long this lunch is."

Yves felt so dazzled that he would have liked to hide his face in his hands. In his bewilderment he tried to find something to say. The sweet biscuits had gone round. He looked at his mother. She was in one of those absent-minded fits which came upon her in company, and had forgotten to move. There was a vague and worried look in her eyes. She had slipped two fingers into the opening of her blouse. While the parish-priest was describing his differences with the Mayor, she was thinking of life at its last gasp, of death, of God's Judgment Seat, and of the breaking-up of family estates.

XII

SATED with good food, the men of the party had gathered under the trees for coffee and liqueurs. Dussol had taken Uncle Xavier aside, and Blanche Frontenac followed them with anxious eyes. She was frightened lest her brother-in-law should let himself be "done". Yves made his way round the house, and then started along the deserted ride which led to the great oak. There was no need for him to go far to be out of reach of their voices, out of smelling distance of their cigars. Wild nature was close at hand. Already, though he had gone but a little way, the trees were unaware that there had been guests to luncheon.

He jumped a ditch. He was slightly drunk (though not as much as he feared he might be, for he had let himself go over the wine). His hide-out, his "hut" was waiting for him. Furze bushes, which the peoples of Les Landes call "jaugues", and bracken, high as a man, surrounded and protected it. It was a place sacred to tears and to the reading of forbidden books, a scene of wild outbursts and of inspiration. There he had flung his challenges to God, there he had prayed and there blasphemed. For some days he had not been near it. Already in the untrodden sand lion-ants had dug their tiny holes. Yves caught an ant, and threw it into one of them. The creature tried to climb out, but the crumbling sides gave way beneath it. From

the bottom of its prison it sent up a little shower of sand.
Barely had it reached the lip of the chasm than it slid down
again. Suddenly it felt itself in the grip of a claw. It fought,
but the monster pulled it slowly underground. Appalling fate!
All around the crickets were shrilling in the still heat of the
lovely day. Dragonflies were hovering, reluctant to settle. The
pink and russet heather, filled with bees, was already sweet
with honey-scent. Yves could see above the sand only the ant's
head and two small, despairing feet. Leaning above this diminu-
tive mystery, the boy of sixteen brooded upon the problem of
evil. The grub that had devised this trap and must, to live and
turn into a butterfly, inflict on ants a ghastly agony; the insect's
terrified clamber from the hole, its failures, and the monster
gripping it . . . all this nightmare was part of the Great Plan.
Yves took a pine-needle and disinterred the lion-ant, a flabby
and now powerless grub. . . . The rescued insect went on its
way, as busy and preoccupied as its companions, and seemingly
oblivious of what it had endured – doubtless because the ordeal
had been natural, had been in accordance with Nature's laws. . . .
But Nature had not reckoned with Yves. With his troubled
heart and his power to suffer, he lay there in a nest of furze.
Had he been the sole human being living and breathing on the
surface of the earth, still, it was enough for him to be there
to destroy the rule of blind necessity, to break the endless
sequence of monsters devouring and devoured. *He* could break
the chain. The least movement of love could break it. Into the
hideous order of the world love could introduce its adorable
power of reversal. *That* was Christ's mystery, and the mystery
of those who take Christ as their model. "For that art thou set
apart . . . I have chosen thee for the upsetting of all things. . . ."
Out loud, the boy said: "It is I who am speaking . . ." (he
pressed his two hands to his sweating face), "it is always ourselves speaking to ourselves. . . ." He tried not to think. High

above him, to the south, into the blue sky rose a covey of wood-pigeons. He followed them with his eyes until they vanished from sight. "Thou knowest full well that I AM who have chosen thee." Yves, squatting on his heels, took a handful of sand and cast it on the empty air. There was a wild look in his eyes, and again and again he cried aloud: "No! . . . no! . . . no!"

"I have chosen thee, have set thee apart from others, have marked thee with my sign."

Yves clenched his fists. This was pure delirium, he told himself: he was flown with wine. He wanted only to be left alone. He wanted no more than to be a boy of his age, just like every other boy of his age. He would know well enough how to escape from solitude.

"Always will I build it up about thee."

"Am I not free? – yes, I am free!" – he cried.

He stood up, and his shadow moved upon the bracken.

"Thou art free to drag through the world a heart which I have not created for the world – free to seek on earth the food for which thou wast not destined, free to try to assuage a hunger which will never find wherewithal to satisfy itself. In no living creature shall it find satisfaction, and thou wilt turn in vain from one to another."

"I am talking to myself," he said again: "I am just like other men: I am their living image."

There was a singing in his ears. A longing for sleep stretched him upon the sand. He lay with his head on his crooked arm. A bee buzzed about him, then flew away to be lost in the spaces of Heaven. . . . The east wind was heavy with the smell of baking bread and sawn wood. He closed his eyes. Flies clung to his face which had a taste of salt. With a sleepy gesture he drove them from him. . . . The sight of him lying there did not worry the evening crickets. A squirrel clambered down the

nearest pine, and, on its way to drink at the stream, passed close
to him. An ant, perhaps the very ant that he had rescued, began
to crawl up his leg with others at its heels. How long would
he have had to stay motionless before they grew bold enough
to eat him?

The freshness of the stream awakened him. He made his
way out of the tangled undergrowth. There were stains of resin
on his coat. He picked the pine-needles from his hair. The
meadow-mist was creeping gradually into the woods, and it
was like the breath from a living mouth in cold weather. As
he turned a corner in the ride, he found himself face to face
with his mother. She was telling her Rosary. She had thrown
an old violet shawl over her party dress. A lace "fall" – "a lovely
thing", as she always called it – adorned her bodice. . . . A long
gold chain and a string of small pearls were secured by a brooch
which carried two large initials, a B and an F, interlaced.

"Where've you been? . . . They were looking for you . . .
it was scarcely polite."

He took his mother's arm and pressed against her.

"I'm frightened of people," he said.

"Frightened of Dussol? frightened of the Cazavieilhs? . . .
My dear boy, you must be mad!"

"They're ogres, mamma."

"I must admit," she said dreamily, "that they haven't left
much."

"Do you think that anything at all will be left of Jean-Louis
in ten years' time? Dussol will swallow him, bit by bit."

"What nonsense you do talk!"

The words were uncompromising, but there was a note of
tenderness in the voice that spoke them.

"You must try to understand me, darling. I want to see Jean-
Louis settled. His home will be your home. As soon as he has
a family life of his own I can depart in peace."

"I won't have you say things like that, mamma!"

"Even after that short little walk I've got to sit down: so, you see there is something in what I say."

She dropped on to the bench which stood under the great oak. Yves saw her slip her hand into her bodice.

"You know it's not malignant. . . . Arnozan has told you that a hundred times."

"So they say . . . but that's not the only thing . . . there are the rheumatic twinges round my heart. I don't think you realize how much suffering I have to put up with. You'd better face the truth, my boy: sooner or later you'll have to. . . ."

Once again he pressed against his mother, and took her broad, worn face between his hands.

"You are here," he said: "you will always be here."

She felt him shiver, and asked whether he felt cold. She covered him with her violet shawl. They snuggled together, both enveloped in the same old woollen wrap.

"You had this shawl when I made my First Communion, mamma . . . it smells just the same."

"Your grandmother brought it back from Salies."

Perhaps for the very last time as a small boy Yves pressed against his mother's living body. At any moment she might disappear. But for centuries and centuries the Hure would flow, and until the end of time the mists would rise from these meadows towards the evening star.

"You who know so much, Yves, tell me – do the spirits in Heaven think of those whom they have left behind on earth? . . . That, at any rate, is what I believe. . . . I can entertain no thought against the Faith . . . but how is it possible to imagine a world in which you, my dear ones, will not be all in all to me?"

Then did Yves assure her that all separate loves would be perfected in the one and only Love, that the heart's affection would be lightened and purified of all that once had muddied it. . . . He was amazed at his own words.

His mother murmured on a sigh:

"Oh, how I pray that none of you will ever be lost!"

They got up, and Yves's mind was full of anxious thoughts, while the old woman, now at peace, leaned on his arm.

"I always tell others that they do not know my darling Yves. Hot-headed you may be, but of all my children you are the one who is nearest to God. . . ."

"No, mamma! – please don't say that! No! no! . . ."

Suddenly he broke from her.

"What's wrong with you? what's the matter?" He walked in front of her, his hands in his pockets, his shoulders hunched. She panted in her effort to keep up with him.

Madame Frontenac was tired out. As soon as dinner was over she went to her room. Since the night was fine, the other members of the family started off for a stroll in the park, but no longer in a compact group. Already, life was loosening the bonds which had held the boys together. . . . Jean-Louis passed Yves at a corner of the path, but neither stopped. The elder wanted to be left alone with his happiness. He was no longer oppressed by a sense of diminution, by a feeling that he had fallen from a high estate. Certain things that Dussol had said about the workers had awakened in him preoccupations which were still at the vague stage. He would do good, in spite of his business associate, would further the coming of a Christian social order. He would not be content with wordy theories, but would do something concrete. Whatever Yves might think, *that* was more important than any amount of speculative philosophy. . . . The smallest act of charity ranks immeasurably higher. . . . Jean-Louis could not live happily on the labour of those who were strangers to happiness. . . . 'I want to help them to build homes that shall be conceived in the image of mine . . .' He saw the gleam of Uncle Xavier's cigar. For a while the two of them walked side by side.

"You're happy, my boy, aren't you? – What did I say?"

Jean-Louis made no attempt to explain to his uncle the nature of the projects which had so filled him with enthusiasm. Nor was it possible for his uncle to put into words his own pleasure at the idea of getting back to Angoulême . . . Joséfa had been disappointed in that matter of the trip, but he would make it all up to her, and at little cost to himself – maybe by doubling her monthly allowance. . . . He would say, "After all, if we'd gone, it would all be over by this time. . . ."

'First of all,' Jean-Louis was thinking, 'before I can even think of anything in the nature of a Mission, there are certain essential reforms to be carried through . . . some form of profit-sharing.' From now on he must shape all his reading to that end.

By the light of the moon they saw José cross the ride from one clump of bushes to another. They could hear the crackle of twigs under his feet. Where was this particular Frontenac off to? – this young fox whom they could have trailed by his scent? . . . In the darkness he was, of all of them, the closest akin to the purely instinctive animal, the young male outcast whose fate it would be never to find the female whom he sought. On he went, treading the dead leaves under foot, tearing his hands on the prickly furze, until at last he reached the Home-Farm which lay just beyond the confines of the park. . . . From somewhere under the pergola a dog growled. The kitchen window stood open. The family was grouped about the table, lit by an oil lamp. José could see in profile the married daughter, the one with a thick neck and a small head. He stood there, munching a leaf of mint, and never taking his eyes from her.

Meanwhile, Yves was making the round of the park for the

third time. Not yet was he conscious of the weariness which soon would fling him, utterly worn out, upon his bed. At dinner he had drunk the wine of feasting to the dregs, and now, feeling wonderfully clear-headed, was casting up the day's balance-sheet, and constructing the framework of that doctrine into the secret freedoms of which Jean-Louis was no longer worthy to be admitted. His state of semi-drunkenness had filled him with a facile sense of genius. He would make no choice. He was under no compulsion to choose. He had been wrong to say "No!" to that urgent voice which might, for all he knew, have been the voice of God. Never would he say "No!" to anybody, and from that refusal to refuse would spring his drama and the tensions out of which his work would grow. All his poetry was to be the expression of a rending struggle – to refuse nothing, never to refuse himself to anything. All imaginative work thrives on pain and passion, drawing from them the sustenance which swells the bud of art. But because the poet is torn and rent, so also is he pardoned. *I know that Thou hast kept for the poet a place in the Legions of the Blest . . .*" The monotonous sound of his voice would have thrilled Uncle Xavier, so like it was to Michel Frontenac's.

Blanche was so tired that she expected to go to sleep as soon as she had blown out her candle. But she could hear the children's footsteps on the gravel. . . . She must remember to send some money to the bailiff at Respide . . . she must find out how her balance stood at the Crédit Lyonnais. . . . October Quarter-Day would soon be coming round. . . . Fortunately, the house-property was still intact. But what did all that matter now! She touched the gland with her fingers. She looked into her heart.

Not one of the Frontenacs on this especial night was visited by the slightest presentiment that for all of them an era was to end with the close of these summer holidays. The long, hot days were already fading into a past to which, as they withdrew, they were carrying, never to be restored, the pure and simple pleasures of a happiness that leaves no stain upon the heart.

Yves, alone, was conscious of a change, but the effect of that knowledge was that, more than all the others, he would build for himself a world of illusion. He saw himself standing on the threshold of a life blazing with inspiration and filled with perilous experience. In fact, though he did not know it, he was about to enter upon a period of squalor. For the next four years his every thought would be dominated by the terrors of examinations. The circles in which he must move would be dim and mediocre. The restlessness of puberty and its petty prurience would set him on a level with his companions and make of him their fellow. The time was fast approaching when his main preoccupation would be how to get his mother to let him have a latchkey, and how to wheedle from her permission to stay out after midnight. He would not be unhappy. At long intervals a whisper from his deeper self would drift to the surface of his life, as from some being shrouded and entombed. At such times he would let his companions go their ways without him. Seated alone at a table in the *Café de Bordeaux*, among the thistles and the shapeless women of the *art nouveau* mosaics, he would start scribbling away on sheets of letter-paper, at top speed, without troubling even to form his writing properly for fear of losing the words which are whispered in the poet's ear once, and once only. Then would come Paris, and the task of developing that other self whom, already, a tiny group of enthusiasts would be already praising to the skies, a group so small, that it would be many years before he awoke to his own importance and took the measure of his victory. A product of the Provinces, an admirer of established reputations, he would, for a long time, fail to realize that his was a reputation of a different kind – that his was a genius born in obscurity, working underground like a mole, and not emerging into the light until much journeying in the unseen depths had been accomplished.

But agony lay in wait for him. How could its horror have been foretold to the Yves Frontenac now leaning at his bed-room window in the mild and moist September darkness? The more his poetry won the hearts of others, the more was he to feel himself impoverished. Strangers would drink of those waters, and only he would know how muddied and befouled had grown the source from which they flowed. That know-ledge would lie at the roots of his self-distrust, causing him to shrink from the clamorous enthusiasm of the Paris world. It would set him for a long time at odds with the editor of one of the most influential of the "advanced" Reviews, and, in the long run, would make him hesitate to collect his poems into a volume.

Yves, at his window, murmured an evening prayer to the tangled darkness of tree-thick Bourideys and the wandering moon. He was ready and eager for all that the future might hold, even if it turned out to be suffering. What he was not ready to face was the shame of long outliving his inspiration, of using subterfuge to keep his fame alive. He could not foresee that one day he would find words to express this drama in a Journal which, after a great war, would be published, nor that he would resign himself to making it public after a long age of silence. That terrible record was to prove the crowning feature of his reputation, and to do more for his fame than all his poems. It was to bring enchantment and a pleasing turmoil into the hearts of a despairing generation. And so it was that, on this September night, God, maybe, saw this young boy rapt in reverie before the sleeping pines, as the starting-point of a strange sequence of cause and effect. The youth who thought himself so proud was very far then from realizing how wide an influence he would exert. Not even vaguely did he dream that the destiny of many would be different from what on earth and in Heaven it might have been, had no Yves Frontenac been born. .

PART TWO

Que les oiseaux et les sources
sont loins! Ce ne peut être que
la fin du monde, en avançant.
                    RIMBAUD

XIII

"FIVE thousand francs worth of debt in three months! Who would ever have dreamed of such a thing in our day, Dussol?"

"Ah, but we, Caussade, had a proper respect for money – we knew how our dear parents had strained and slaved to put something by. *We* were brought up to believe in saving. 'Discipline – Work – Economy' – such was my admirable father's motto."

Blanche Frontenac broke in on them.

"It's not you we're discussing, but José."

She was sorry now that she had taken Dussol and her brother-in-law into her confidence. . . . When Jean-Louis discovered what was going on, he had had to mention it to Dussol, because José had been pledging the firm's credit, and Dussol had insisted on calling a family-council. But Madame Frontenac and Jean-Louis had been against saying anything to Uncle Xavier. He had a bad heart, and this blow might make it worse. Why, Blanche wondered, had Alfred Caussade been brought into the business at all? Jean-Louis regretted it as much as she did.

The young man sat facing his mother. Office life had aged him. His hair was already receding, although he was not more than twenty-three.

"The boy really must be a half-wit"—said Alfred Caussade – "I gather that quite a lot of fellows have had this woman for nothing . . . ever seen her, Dussol?"

"Once" – replied Dussol – "and not from choice, I can assure you! Madame Dussol wanted to go to the Apollo, just to see what the place is like, you know, and I didn't feel I had

any right to refuse to take her. Naturally, we had a box – we
didn't want to be seen. The way that creature Stéphane Paros
danced! – not a stitch on her legs! . . ."

Uncle Alfred's eyes gleamed. He leaned closer to the
speaker:

"I'm told that sometimes . . ."

The rest of the sentence was inaudible. Dussol took off his
pince-nez and threw back his head.

"It's only fair to say," he went on, "that she was wearing
some sort of close-fitting garment on the upper part of her
body – a very flimsy sort of affair, to be sure, still, it did cover
her. . . . She always does, I'm told. . . . You can't suppose that
I should have exposed Madame Dussol . . . Still, bare legs are
bad enough in all conscience. . . ."

"*And* bare feet . . ." put in Alfred Caussade.

"Oh, feet!" – and Dussol made an indulgent grimace.

"Speaking for myself . . ." – declared Alfred with a sort of
embarrassed eagerness – "I find bare feet more disgusting than
anything else. . . ."

Blanche interrupted him angrily:

"It's you who are being disgusting, Alfred!"

He protested, tugging at his beard, and smoothing it with
his hand:

"My dear Blanche! . . ."

"It's time we reached some kind of decision. What do you
advise, Dussol?"

"Send him away, dear lady. The sooner he leaves and the
further he goes the better. My own choice would be Winnipeg
. . . but I know you won't agree to that. . . . We need somebody in Norway . . . the salary won't be large, but there's
nothing like roughing it to teach a young man the value of
money. . . . D'you agree, Jean-Louis?"

The latter replied, without looking at his partner, that he

was certainly of the opinion that José ought to be got out of Bordeaux. Blanche looked across at her eldest son:

"Oh, but . . . but . . . we've lost Yves already!"

"You should never, dear lady, have let *him* out of your sight!" exclaimed Dussol. "I only wish you had asked my advice. There was no earthly reason why he should go to Paris. You're not, surely, going to tell me that his work made it necessary? I know pretty well what you think about his so-called work! – in that direction maternal affection has certainly not blinded you – you've got too much sound commonsense! I scarcely think that I am destroying any illusions you may harbour, when I say that his literary future . . . and, mind you, I know what I am talking about, I have taken great pains to keep abreast of his productions, even to the extent of reading some of them aloud to Madame Dussol, though I must admit, she very soon begged for mercy! . . . I know, of course, that you'll tell me he has received a certain amount of encouragement . . . but what sort of encouragement, may I ask? Jean-Louise showed me a letter from a Monsieur Gide, but who *he* is nobody knows. There is an economist of that name, to be sure, but unfortunately, it didn't come from him! . . ."

Though Jean-Louis had long realized that his mother never minded contradicting herself, and that logic was not one of her strong points, he was frankly amazed to hear her now opposing Dussol with the very arguments he had himself used against her only the evening before!

"It would be a great deal better if you didn't talk about what you cannot possibly understand. His poems are not written for people like you – who approve only of what is familiar to them, what they have already come across somewhere else. The new shocks them. Isn't that so, Jean-Louis? Yves tells me that even Racine shocked his contemporaries."

"You're not going to tell me that the glories of Racine can

be mentioned in the same breath as the outpourings of *that* young cub!"

"Let me advise you, my poor friend, to give your mind to timber and to leave poetry alone! Poetry is not your concern – any more than it is mine" – she added, in an effort of appeasement – for he was swelling like a turkey-cock, and his neck was turning bright red.

"Madame Dussol and I are at great pains to keep ourselves up to date. I was one of the earliest patrons of the *Panbiblion* library, and my subscription covers periodicals as well as books – we make it a point to know what is going on in the world of the higher journalism. Only the other day, one of my colleagues at the Chamber of Commerce was saying that what makes Madame Dussol's conversation so delightful is that she has read everything, and has such a truly amazing memory that she can tell you the plot of a novel or a play which she hasn't looked at for years, just as though she has only just been reading it. He went so far as to add – and I thought it very wittily put – "A woman like that is a walking library . . ."

"She is to be envied" – said Blanche: "my own memory is like a sieve; nothing sticks in it."

This piece of self-criticism was intended to disarm Dussol.

"Whew!" she exclaimed with a sigh when the two elderly gentlemen had departed.

She drew her chair to the fire. The radiators were full on, but she had never, since moving to this house, got used to the central heating. For her, not being cold meant seeing a fire and roasting her legs. She was in a mood of self-pity. So now she must lose José! – and next year he wanted to enlist as a volunteer in Morocco. . . . She ought never to have let Yves go from her! What Dussol had said was true – though not for anything in the world would she have admitted as much to him . . . the boy could just as well have done his writing in Bordeaux. She felt convinced that he was merely idling away his time in Paris.

"It was you who put the idea into his head, Jean-Louis. He would never have left us of his own accord."

"That's not fair, mamma! You know that since the girls have been married and you have come to live with them in this house, you think of nothing but their family affairs and their children. All that's perfectly right and proper, but Yves would have felt utterly lost in this nursery atmosphere."

"Lost! . . . didn't I sit up every night with him when he had congestion of the lungs?"

"Yes, and he said he liked being ill because it was only then that he felt you were really close to him. . . ."

"He's an ungrateful young scamp, that's the long and the short of it!"

Jean-Louis made no reply, and she went on:

"Tell me, what do you really think he's doing with himself in Paris?"

"Working away at his book, of course, seeing all he can of other writers, talking of what interests him, making contact with editors and people in the literary world . . . all that sort of thing."

Madame Frontenac shook her head: "all that sort of thing" conveyed nothing to her. What she wanted to know was the kind of life he was living. She was afraid that he had lost all his principles. . . .

"But there is a deep note of mysticism in everything he writes . . ." (Jean-Louis flushed scarlet) . . . "Only the other day Thibaudet wrote that his poetry postulates a metaphysic. . . ."

"That's just a lot of words . . ." she broke in. "What are metaphysics worth, if he doesn't take Easter Communion? . . .

a mystic indeed! . . . a young man who absents himself from the Sacraments! . . . really!"

Jean-Louis said nothing, and she went on:

"When you see him on your trips to Paris, what does he talk about? Does he just tell you of the people he's been meeting – and nothing else? surely, as brother to brother . . ."

"Brothers," said Jean-Louis, "have a certain intuition, a certain understanding, about one another, but only up to a point . . . they don't share their secrets. . . ."

"What exactly do you mean? – you're too complicated for me. . . ."

Leaning forward, with her elbows on her knees, Blanche poked the fire.

"What are we to do about José, mamma?"

"Oh, what it is to have sons! . . . Luckily, you, at least . . ."

She looked at him. Was he really as happy as she liked to think? His shoulders carried a heavy load of responsibility, and he did not always get on with Dussol. She felt compelled to admit that sometimes he did not show himself to be prudent, or even possessed of ordinary common-sense. . . . It is all very well for an employer to have a social conscience, but, as Dussol said, it is only when one comes to balance the books that one realizes how much a social conscience costs. She had had to admit that Dussol had been right when he had opposed Jean-Louis's project of setting up "Factory Councils" in which representatives of Workers and Management should sit down together round a table, and when he had set his face against a system of Arbitration Boards, the working of which Jean-Louis had tried to explain to him, though without success. In the matter of one innovation, however, Dussol had finally yielded, and it was the one which, really, was closest to his young partner's heart. "Let him try it out", Dussol had said.

"No doubt it'll cost a pretty penny, but he's got to sow his wild oats some time!"

Jean-Louis's great idea was to give the workers an interest in the business. With Dussol's permission he called them together and explained the scheme. What he proposed was to issue shares to all his workers in proportion to the length of each man's service. Dussol's common-sense attitude was completely vindicated. The men regarded the whole thing as a huge joke. Before a month was out they had sold all the shares allotted to them. "I told him again and again," said Dussol, "that that was what would happen, and now he's seen for himself. I don't regret the cost. He knows at least the kind of people he's dealing with, and he won't be victimized a second time. The really funny thing is that the men respect me for being as hard as nails. They know they can't get round me. I talk their language, and they like me, whereas he, with all his socialistic notions, strikes them as being proud and aloof. It's always me they come to when they want anything."

"If you'd really rather let José stay on in Bordeaux" – said Jean-Louis – "I can't see any real reason why he shouldn't. This Paros woman has sent me word by her man of business that she has got no designs on him, and has never accepted anything from him but flowers. It was scarcely her fault if José always insisted on footing the bill when they dined together. . . . She believed him to be a rich man. . . . In any case, she is leaving Bordeaux next week. . . . All the same, I think it would do him good to have a change of scene until his time for military service comes round. . . . Some other woman might get her claws into him. . . . But I don't at all agree with Dussol that we ought to keep him short of money. . . ."

Madame Frontenac shrugged her shoulders:

"Of course not. When they were all talking just now about

it being such a good thing for young men to rough it, I didn't say anything, because I didn't want to make a fuss . . . but really, what an idea!"

"Shall I go and fetch him? he's waiting upstairs in his room."

"Yes, and switch on the light."

A ceiling-lamp provided gloomy illumination for the Empire room with its faded wallpaper.

Jean-Louis turned with José.

"This is what we've decided, old chap. . . ."

The culprit remained standing in the shadows with lowered eyes. He looked stockier than his brothers, "low on his feet", but with a great spread of shoulder. He had a dark, swarthy face which showed blue to the cheek-bones. Blanche noted in the young man the same power of withdrawal which had marked the schoolboy when she used to hear him his home-work in the melancholy evenings of the years gone by. He had never listened to a word she said. No matter how much she might implore and threaten, he had always managed, in the most extraordinary way, to escape into a world of his own, to absent himself. Just as when, in his boyhood, he had buried himself in delightful dreams of summer holidays at Bourideys; just as, later on, he had had no thoughts but for the life of a trapper, and was quite capable of spending whole winter nights in a "hideout", watching for wild duck – so now, the whole force of his awareness, of his desire, had become centred, at one fell swoop, upon a woman – a perfectly ordinary woman, by no means fresh, who was touring the Provinces with a sort of Frégoli act (*The Dancer of Seville* – *The Houri* – *The Nautch-Girl*). A friend had introduced her to him after the perform-ance. There had been a party of them in a night-club. That evening, for the first and only time, he had found favour in the lady's eyes, and had become wildly infatuated. She had filled his world to the exclusion of everyone, and everything, else.

The office, in those days, had seen little of him, but Jean-Louis had taken over his work as well as his own. Finally, his timid but mulish obstinacy had got on the lady's nerves. . . .

And now, here he was, standing between his mother and his brother, with a blank, impenetrable look upon his face.

"These debts of yours are a serious matter . . ." said his mother. "But I don't want you to think that it's the money that chiefly worries me. What matters to me, above all else, is the wild way of life into which you have fallen . . . I have always had confidence in my sons, have always believed that they would eschew base actions . . . and now, you, José . . ."

Had her words shaken him? He sat down on the divan with the light full in his face. He had grown thinner: even his temples looked hollow. In an expressionless voice he asked when he was to leave.

"In January, after the Christmas holidays," she said, and he replied:

"The sooner the better."

He was taking it all very well. Everything, Blanche told herself, would be for the best. All the same, she was far from being easy in her mind, and sought for reassurance. It did not escape her that Jean-Louis, too, was looking at his younger brother. Anyone other than themselves would have taken comfort in the young man's quietness. But both mother and brother knew what they were up against. This particular kind of suffering was something with which they were familiar. They were linked physically with the despair before them, which, being a child's, was despair in its worst form, impossible to interpret, and proof against any obstacle of reason, self-interest, or ambition. . . . The elder brother kept his eyes firmly fixed upon the prodigal. The mother rose to her feet. She went across to José, took his face in her two hands, as though to waken him, as though to rouse him from hypnotic slumber:

"José, look at me."

She spoke in a tone of command, and he, with a child's impatience, shook his head, closed his eyes, and sought to free himself from her clasp. In the hard and secret look of her son's face, Blanche saw what she herself had never known – the agony of love. He'd get over it . . . it wouldn't last long . . . only, he had got to reach the further bank and not drown in mid-stream. This boy of hers had always frightened her. When he was young she had never known, with certainty, how he would react. If only he would say something! if only he would complain! But no, there he sat, with his jaw clenched, presenting to his mother the burned-up face of a child of Les Landes (perhaps, long ago, some woman of the family had been seduced by one of those Catalans who lived by selling smuggled matches). His eyes blazed, but their fire was dark, and revealed nothing. Then Jean-Louis, approaching in his turn, took the other by the shoulders and shook him, though without roughness. Several times he said – "José, old man, José, old boy" . . . and succeeded where his mother had failed. He made his brother cry. The mother's tenderness was so familiar to him that it could no longer produce any reaction: but never, until now, had Jean-Louis shown such tenderness. So unexpected was it that he had, perforce, to yield to his surprise. The tears burst from his eyes, and he clung to his brother as though he had been a drowning man. Instinctively, Madame Frontenac had turned away her face and gone back to the fire. She heard the stammered words; she heard the convulsive sobbing. She leaned above the fire, her hands clasped across her mouth.

The two brothers approached her.

"He's going to be sensible, mamma, he's promised."

She drew her unhappy son into her arms. "Darling, you'll never look like this again, will you?"

Once more, and once only, would that terrible expression show upon his face, and that, towards the end of a fine, warm day in late August, at Mourmelon, in 1915, between two army huts. No one would notice it, not even the friend seeking to dissipate his fears:

"There's going to be a terrific artillery preparation. Everything'll be smashed to pieces, and there'll be nothing left for us to do but walk forward with our hands in our pockets and our rifles slung . . ."

To him José Frontenac would show just such a face, drained of all hope, though then it would no longer waken fear in anybody.

XIV

JEAN-LOUIS hurried home. He lived only a few yards away, in the rue Lafaurie de Montbadon. He was eager to tell Madeleine everything before dinner. Yves had given him a disgust of the little house which they had furnished with such loving care. "You're neither a budding dentist, nor a doctor just starting in practice" – his brother had said. "There's no reason in the world why you should display on the mantelpiece, the walls, and even on special stands, the loathsome presents with which your friends have inundated you." Jean-Louis had protested, though half-heartedly: but now it was with Yves's eyes that he saw the crowded cupids in biscuit-china, the art-bronzes, and the Austrian terra-cottas.

"Baby's feverish," said Madeleine. She was sitting beside the cradle. The country girl, transplanted to the city, had thickened.

With her broad shoulders and powerful neck she looked no longer young. Perhaps she was with child? A blue and swollen vein showed just above her breast.

"How much temperature?"

"99·2. She sicked up her four o'clock bottle."

"Did you put the thermometer up her rectum? 99·2's not fever, especially at night."

"It is. Dr. Chatard said it was."

"He meant the under-arm temperature."

"It *is* fever, I tell you: not much, I know, but still, fever."

He made an impatient gesture and leaned over the cradle which smelt of wet straw mattress and sicked-up milk. He kissed the child, and it started to cry.

"Your beard's pricking her."

"Fresh as a peach," he said.

He began walking up and down the room, hoping that she would ask him about José. But she never put, unprompted, the questions that he wanted. He should have known that by this time: but he was always caught off-guard.

She said:

"You'd better start dinner without me."

"Because of the child?"

"Yes: I want to wait until she's asleep."

He felt thoroughly annoyed. This *would* be the evening when they were to have cheese soufflé, which has got to be eaten the moment it comes out of the oven. Madeleine must have re-membered it – she was country-bred to her bones, brought up with an almost religious regard for family meal-times, and a healthy respect for food – because almost before Jean-Louis had spread his napkin, she had joined him. No good, he thought, waiting for her to speak first. It was obvious that she wouldn't ask him what had happened.

"Aren't you at all curious, darling?"

She was half asleep, and the eyes she turned to him were puffy.

"Curious about what?"

"José," he said. "It was quite a business. Dussol and Uncle Xavier didn't dare insist on Winnipeg . . . so it's got to be Norway."

"That won't be much of a punishment. . . . I suppose he can get his duck-shooting as easily there as here, and that's all he really cares about."

"Are you quite sure? . . . I wish you could have seen him . . . he loves her, you know" – and Jean-Louis went very red.

"What, a creature like that?"

"You shouldn't jeer at him" – and then, "I wish you could have seen him," he said again.

Madeleine's smile was knowing and unkind. She shrugged her shoulders, but said no more. She wasn't a Frontenac, he reflected, so what was the use of going on about it? She wouldn't understand. She wasn't a Frontenac. He tried to recollect precisely *how* José had looked, to remember the stammered words. That secret passion . . .

"Danièle very sweetly came to tea with me. She brought the pattern for that brassière – you know, the one I told you about."

The solid, sensible Jean-Louis could not but envy folly carried to such desperate lengths. He felt disgusted with himself, and looked across at his wife, who was rolling her bread into a pellet.

"What did you say?"

"Nothing . . . I didn't speak. What's the use? You don't listen to anything I say. You never answer."

"You said that Danièle had come to tea, didn't you?"

"If you promise not to repeat it, I'll tell you something. I rather think her husband has had enough of this living with your mother. He means to move as soon as he gets a rise."

"But they can't do that! It was partly because of them that mamma bought the house. They don't pay a penny of rent."

"That's the only thing that keeps them there. She's a very exhausting person to live with. . . . You know that well enough, you've told me so yourself a hundred times."

"Have I? Yes, I suppose I may have . . ."

"Besides, she'll still have Marie. *Her* husband's a great deal more patient, and has more of an eye to the main chance. He'll never willingly break up such a comfortable arrangement."

Jean-Louis saw his mother in the rather humiliating position of an old country-woman bandied about between her various children. Madeleine would not let the subject drop.

"I'm very fond of her, and she dotes on me. But I know that I couldn't live with her – I just couldn't."

"She, on the other hand, could quite easily live with you."

There was uneasiness in the look which Madeleine turned on her husband.

"You're not angry, are you? It doesn't make me love her any the less. . . . It's just a question of differences in character. . . ."

He got up, went round the table, and gave his wife a kiss. It was his way of saying that he was sorry for what he had been thinking. Just as they were preparing to leave the room, the servant came in with two letters. On one of the envelopes Jean-Louis recognized Yves's handwriting, and he slipped it into his pocket. He asked Madeleine's permission to open the other.

DEAR SIR AND BENEFACTOR

I take up my pen to let you know as our youngest is agoing to take her first communion Thursday come two weeks and she knows all her prayers and her father and me when we sees her saying of her prayers at night and morning we feel quite soft and silly but annoyed too along of knowing as a festival costs a lot even when its for the Good God and we owing a tidy lot of money here and there. But as I said to my husband your benefactors not the sort to leave you in the lurch you being one as kept your shares instead of selling them off to buy drink like some did and there wasnt not one of them sober for a month after the shares was given out which it was a black shame and those as understood your kind thought being called scabs and arselickers and other things as respect for good manners wont let me write on paper. But as my husband says when a chaps got a boss like that its up to him to show himself worthy by understanding all the good things as he intends to do for the workers. . . .

Jean-Louis tore the letter up, and passed his hand several times over his nose and mouth.

"Do stop that nervous trick of yours," said Madeleine, and added: "I'm absolutely dropping! Heavens! it's only nine o'clock. You won't stay up too late, will you? . . . and do, please, undress in the other room."

Jean-Louis loved his library. Yves's critical comments carried no weight there. It contained nothing but books: even the mantelpiece was covered with them. He closed the door with care, sat down at his table, and balanced his brother's letter on his outstretched hand. He was delighted to find that it felt heavier than usual. He opened it, taking great pains not to tear the envelope. As a good Frontenac should, Yves began by giving news of Uncle Xavier, with whom he lunched regularly every Thursday. . . . The thought of one of his nephews settling in Paris had given the poor man the fright of his life, and he had done everything he could to dissuade Yves from taking such a step. The Frontenacs had pretended not to know why he was so disapproving of the plan. "He is less worried now" – wrote Yves – "because he has discovered that Paris is large enough to make it extremely unlikely that a nephew will run up against his uncle when the latter is out with a lady. . . . Yes, that is the long and short of it. I saw them together the other day in the street. In fact, I followed them for a bit, at a safe distance. She is big and blowzy and blonde and must have been quite a good looker twenty years ago. Would you believe it, they headed straight for a Duval[1] – and I've no doubt he'd bought himself a cheap cigar. When he takes *me* out we always go to Prunier's, and he invariably offers me a Bock or a Henry Clay with the coffee. But that, of course, is because I'm a Frontenac. . . . D'you know, I've actually been to see Barrès! . . ." He went on to describe this visit at length. The evening before, a friend had passed on to him something the Master had said to the effect that the whole thing was an awful bore because he'd have to be careful not to "disappoint young Frontenac" . . . and that had put Yves in a cold sweat. "I don't think I was quite as nervous as the Great Man, though pretty nearly! We left the house together, and as soon as we were in the street the specialist of the human heart thawed a bit. He said . . . I mustn't forget a single one of his precious words . . . he said . . ."

But it was not what Barrès had said that interested Jean-Louis. He read rapidly through this part of the letter, anxious to get on to where Yves should begin to describe his life in Paris, his work, his hopes, the men and the women among whom he lived. He turned a page, and could not keep back an exclamation of annoyance. Yves had carefully erased every line! The same on the back, the same on the page that followed. Nor had he been content with merely crossing out what he had written. Each word had been completely obliterated under a dense tangle of squiggles. Perhaps, beneath this passionate deletion all the secrets of a younger brother might lie con-

[1] The Paris equivalent of an A.B.C.—Translator.

cealed! There must, said Jean-Louis to himself, be some way of getting at the text . . . there would almost certainly be specialists in this sort of investigation . . . but, no, he couldn't possibly hand over one of Yves's letters to a stranger. He remembered that there was a magnifying-glass lying about somewhere on his table (another wedding-present!), and began, with its aid, to peer at each concealed word with as much eager intentness as though the fate of the country hung upon his success. But all the magnifying-glass could do was to show him how Yves had gone about the business of foiling just this sort of attempt. Not only had he linked his words by inserting arbitrary letters between them, he had gone to the trouble of making down-strokes where none should be. . . . After working away for an hour, the elder brother had achieved only the most mediocre results. But, at least, Yves's intense efforts to render these pages unreadable were proof of the importance which he attached to them. Jean-Louis sat with his hands on the table. He could hear in the dark and silent street two men talking at the tops of their voices. From the Cours Balguérie came the clanging of the last tram. He stared with tired eyes at the mysterious letter. . . . If he took the car and drove all night, he could be with his brother before noon next day. . . . But he could set off alone like that only if he had some business excuse, and he had none. He had been to Paris three times in a single fortnight when a few thousand francs had been in question, but now that his brother's very safety might be threatened, no one would understand his behaving in so extraordinary a fashion. But threatened by what?

Had Jean-Louis been able to decipher Yves's suppressed intimacies, he would probably have been very considerably disappointed. Discretion rather than shame had dictated the younger brother's cautionary action. 'Of what possible interest can all this be to him?' – he had thought: 'and in any case he wouldn't understand' . . . This latter judgment implied no contempt. The fact of the matter was that when he was away from the members of his family, he thought of them as all compact of innocent simplicity. The people with whom he knocked about in Paris seemed to him to belong to some strange species between which and his country-bred relatives there could be no possible contact. "You just wouldn't know what they were talking about" – was what he had written (not knowing that before the letter was finished he would have scratched all this part out): "they jabber at such a rate, and make so many allusions to people whose nicknames and sexual peculiarities one is assumed to know backwards. I'm always two or three sentences behind, and laugh five minutes after the rest of them. But, since it's the general view that I'm some sort of a genius, this slowness in the uptake is all part of the picture they've made of me, and goes down on the credit-side. Most of them, as a matter of fact, have never read a word I've written, though they pretend to have a complete knowledge of my work. It's me they like, not my productions. Dear old Jean-Louis, it never occurred to us simple Bordeaux folk that the mere fact of being twenty would strike people like that as nothing short of a miracle! We just didn't realize how rich we were! In our homely circle youth isn't rated nearly so high. *We* regard it as the awkward age, the time of fluff and down, of pimples and boils, of moist hands and general grubbiness. The people hereabouts take a more flattering view. Boils don't last. Twenty-four hours is enough to turn you into a representative of the legendary Young. Sometimes a woman will say that she is mad about your poems, that she longs to hear you read them, and her bosom will rise and fall with such a gust of sighs that you'd think she could play the bellows to any fire. This year all doors have opened to my 'marvellous gift of youth' – even very exclusive doors. But literature is a mere excuse, there as elsewhere. No one really cares two hoots about what I *do*, nor understands it. That's not what they're after. All they care about is 'personalities'. I'm a personality, and so would you be, though you mightn't think it. Fortunately, these ogres and ogresses have no teeth left, and are reduced to devouring you with their eyes. They've no idea where I come from, and it wouldn't so much as occur to them to enquire whether or not I've got a mother. I could hate them for no better reason than that they have never asked me for news of mamma. They haven't the least conception what it means to be a Frontenac – even without the particle. The grandeur of the Frontenac 'mystery' is something they have never known. I might be the son of a convict and come straight from prison – it wouldn't make the slightest difference, except that it might give them an added kick. . . . It's enough for them that I am twenty years old, that I wash my hands and the rest of my body, and that I have what they call a 'position' in the literary world, or enough of one to explain my presence – along with Ambassadors and Members of the Institute – at their sumptuous tables – at which, for all their sumptuousness, the wines are badly served, too cold, and in glasses that are too small. . . . As mamma would say, one's only got time for a gulp and a swallow. . . ."

It was at this point that Yves had broken off and, on second thoughts, obliterated what he had written. Nor had it occurred to him that, by so doing, he ran the risk of adding considerably to his brother's bewilderment. Jean-Louis sat and stared at the hieroglyphics. Taking advantage of the fact that he was alone in the room, he surrendered to his nervous trick, and passed his cupped hand slowly over his nose, moustache and lips. . . .

After slipping Yves's letter into his note-case he looked at his watch. Madeleine must be growing impatient. He allowed himself another ten minutes of solitude and silence, took up a book, opened it, closed it again. Was his proclaimed liking for poetry just a pretence? He never, nowadays, seemed to want to read any. But then, he read less and less of anything. Yves had said: 'You're quite right not to clutter up your memory . . . we'd all be much better off if we could forget all the odds and ends we were fools to let ourselves be crammed with. . . ." But Yves said such a lot of things! . . . Since he'd gone to live in Paris one could never be sure whether he was serious or not – probably he didn't know himself.

Jean-Louis noticed the gleam of the bedside lamp showing from under the door. It was a wordless reproach, which meant: "You've kept me from going to sleep. I'd rather lie here waiting for you than be woken up." All the same, he undressed as quietly as possible, and went into the bedroom.

It was very large, and, despite Yves's habit of poking fun at it, Jean-Louis always felt a slight thrill each time he crossed the threshold. The darkness hid the wedding-presents, blurring the outlines of the bronze ornaments and assorted cupids. The furniture was shadowy and vague. The cradle, attached to the immense bed, looked like the basket of a balloon, hanging suspended, as though the child's breathing had been sufficient to inflate the simple curtains.

Madeleine cut Jean-Louis's excuses short.

"I've not been bored," she said: "I've been thinking."

"What about?"

"José," she said.

His mood softened. Just when he had given up all hope, here she was broaching, unprompted, the subject that was nearest to his heart.

"I've hit on the very person for him . . . now don't say 'no' before you've thought about it seriously. . . . Cécile, Cécile Filhot, I mean. She's rich, she's been brought up in the country and is used to men leaving the house before sunrise on a day's shooting, and going to bed at eight. She knows that that kind of man is never at home. She would make him thoroughly happy. I heard him say once that he admired her, that he liked 'great solid women' – those were his very words."

"Oh, but he'd never agree . . . besides, he's still got his three years of military service to do . . . they'll start in twelve months' time . . . he's set his heart on Morocco or one of the Southern Algerian regiments."

"Perhaps, but don't you see that if he were engaged, that'd be a tie. Perhaps papa could wangle it so's he'd get his discharge after a year, as he did in the case of . . ."

"Madeleine, please! . . ."

She bit her lip. The child uttered a faint whimper. She stretched out her arm, and the cradle began to creak like a mill. Jean-Louis was thinking about José's wish to serve in Morocco (it had come to him after reading one of Psichari's books) . . . ought they to encourage him, or try to put a spoke in his wheel?

Suddenly he said:

"I must say it mightn't be at all a bad idea to get him married."

He was thinking of José, but also of Yves. Only in some such room as this, warm and smelling of milk, with its hangings and its padded furniture, a small bundle of wailing life, and a young and fecund woman, could the Frontenac brothers, chased from the family nest and far dispersed, no longer shielded from life by holiday pine-trees and the protective boundaries of a steamy park, find ultimate refuge. Driven from the Paradise of childhood, exiled from its meadow fastnesses, from its bright alders and the streams that wound among the phallic fern, only in some place of hangings and old chairs and cradles, could they find a spot in which to dig their little burrows. . . .

And yet it was this same Jean-Louis, so eager to circle his brothers with protection, and to keep them from the world, who, under the threat of coming war, was strengthening his muscles with daily bouts of exercise. He was concerned to know whether he could get himself transferred from the auxiliary to the fighting forces. But life went on among the Frontenacs as though there were some bond that knit the love of brother for brother with the love of their mother for them all. Rather it was as though those two and differing loves sprang from the same source. Jean-Louis felt for the younger ones, and even for José whose eyes were set so lovingly on Africa, something of the same unquiet and almost agonized solicitude as moved their mother. Tonight, especially, had he felt it, when José's unspoken clamour of despair, and the silence that descends before the storm, had shaken him, though less, perhaps, than Yves's illegibilities. That other letter, too, that begging-letter from a workman's wife, so similar to others that had reached him, had struck deep into his sensibility, and kept a wound wide open. Not yet could he resign himself to taking men as they are. Their crude flatteries got on his nerves, and, even more, their clumsy feigning of religious feelings. These things made him feel ill. He remembered with peculiar vivid-ness the case of an eighteen-year-old boy who had wanted to be baptized. He had himself undertaken his instruction, work-ing at the task with love, only to find, a few days later, that this "godson" had already been baptized through the good offices of a Protestant organization, and had made off with their funds. He knew, of course, that this had been a single, isolated instance, and that there are plenty of good and sincere persons in the world. But, as luck would have it (or, rather, some lack of psychological awareness in himself, an inability to judge his fellow men) he was always being landed in such scrapes. His natural shyness was looked on as aloof superiority. It frightened off the simple, but not the hypocrites and flatterers.

Lying on his back, he gazed at the ceiling in the dim light of the lamp and felt his powerlessness to change the destiny of others. His two brothers would accomplish the work to which they had been called, and, after much wandering, would reach, infallibly, the place at which they were expected, the place where Someone watched for them. . . .

"Madeleine," he asked suddenly, "do you think that one can ever do anything for other people?"

She turned to him a face half dulled with sleep, and pushed the hair from her eyes.

"What d'you say?"

"I mean, do you believe that if one tried hard enough, one could ever transform another's destiny, however little?"

"Oh, that's all you ever think about, changing other people, moving them about, giving them different ideas from the ones they've got. . . ."

"Perhaps" (he was speaking to himself) "all I succeed in doing is to strengthen their natural tendencies. When I think I'm holding them back, they gather themselves for a forward spring along the path traced out for them. And it is usually in the very opposite direction from that in which I want to see them go . . . ."

She stifled a yawn.

"What's the use, darling?"

When, at the Last Supper, the Saviour spoke his sorrowful and tender words to Judas, they merely seemed to drive him to the door and set him on his destined way more quickly.

"Do you realize what time it is . . . after midnight? . . . You'll never be able to get up in the morning."

He switched off the lamp, and lay in the darkness as though at the bottom of the sea, with the vast weight of the waters pressing him down. His head swam with a sense of solitude and anguish. He remembered suddenly that he had forgotten to say his prayers. Grown man though he was, he did precisely as he would have done when he was ten years old. He got up quietly and knelt down beside the bed, burying his face in the sheets. Not a whisper troubled the silence. Not a sound revealed the presence in the room of a woman and a sleeping child. The atmosphere was heavy with a confusion of smells, for Madeleine, like all country folk, had a horror of the night air. Her husband had had to resign himself to sleeping with closed windows. He began by invoking the Holy Spirit: *Veni, Sancte Spiritus, reple tuorum corda fidelium et tui amoris in eis ignem accende* . . . But even while his lips were shaping the lovely formula, he was conscious only of the peace he knew so well, the peace that, in himself, bubbled up everywhere, like a river at its rising, flooding his being, overcoming all resistance, like waters in spate. From past experience he knew that he must not attempt to think, nor yield to the false humility which finds expression in such words as – "It doesn't mean anything: it is a mere surface emotion. . . ." No, he must say nothing at all, must simply accept. Nothing of his former anguish remained. . . . What madness to believe that the apparent consequence of our efforts is of the slightest importance. . . . What counts is the effort itself, the effort to hold the tiller firm, to get the ship back on to its true course – that especially. . . . The unknown, the unforeseeable, the unimaginable fruits of our actions will one day be revealed in the light, those rejected fruits, piled high upon the ground, that we dare not offer. . . . He made a brief examination of conscience. Yes, tomorrow morning he would be in a fit state to take Communion. . . . He let himself relax. He knew precisely where he was, and was still aware of the room's peculiar atmosphere. One thought, and one thought only, gnawed at him – that at this very moment he was yielding to a movement of pride, was seeking a pleasure. . . .

"But, were it thou, Oh Lord . . ."

The silence of the countryside had welled up over the town. Jean-Louis lay listening to the ticking of his watch. In the darkness, he could just make out Madeleine's humped shoulder. His mind was perfectly clear, yet nothing distracted it from the essential. Certain problems rose up within his field of consciousness, but, once resolved, vanished. For instance, thinking of Madeleine, he saw with blinding clarity, that women carry within themselves a world of feelings richer by far than ours, though they lack the power to interpret and express them, and that this constitutes a seeming inferiority. Similarly, with the "People" . . . Their limited vocabulary . . . Jean-Louis had a feeling that he was moving from infinity towards the earth, that his steps were no longer uncertain, that he had touched solid ground, that he was walking on the sea-shore, that he was moving away from his love. He made the sign of the cross, slid down beneath the sheets, and closed his eyes. The sound of a ship's siren on the river scarcely reached him. The rumble of the early market-carts did not awaken him.

XV

THE driver turned his head, without diminishing his speed, and shouted:

"What about stopping at Bordeaux for lunch?"

The Englishman, squashed between the two women at the back of the car, put a question:

"The *Chapon Fin*, eh?"

The young man at the wheel gave him a black look. Yves Frontenac, who was sitting beside him, expressed his nervousness:

"Geo, do, for Heaven's sake, keep your eye on the road . . . look . . . there's a child!"

What a fool he'd been to start out with this car-load of strangers! Three days earlier, he had been dining in Paris at the house of the American woman whose name he could never remember and would, in any case, have been incapable of pronouncing. . . . He had been more than usually "brilliant" (it was generally agreed that he was not to be relied upon: he could, on occasion, be the gloomiest of guests). "You're in luck's way," Geo had said. He was one of Yves's admirers, and was responsible for his presence there: "Frontenac's on top of his form." The Pommery had created a warm feeling of friendship between these various persons who scarcely knew each other. Their hostess was leaving next morning for Guéthary. A three days' trip, no more. She suggested that they should all go with her. It would be too awful to have to separate. From now on, they had got to stick together. . . . The June night was warm. As luck would have it, none of the men was in evening dress. It was simply a question of getting the car round and starting off. They could have baths when they got there. . . .

At Bordeaux, after lunch, Yves had paid his mother a surprise visit. He found her alone. At sight of her son, whom she was not expecting, she went very pale. He kissed her ashen cheeks. The window of the Empire drawing-room was wide open on the noisy smelly street. He could only spare her, he said, a quarter of an hour, because his friends were in a hurry to press on to Guéthary. They wouldn't be stopping in Bordeaux on the way back. Not that it really mattered, because, in less than three weeks he would be coming down to spend a whole month with his mother (her married children had rented a villa out on the Harbour, and there wouldn't be room for her). She had decided to go to Respide, on the slopes above the Garonne, and there wait for Yves to join her, instead of in the muggy heat of Bourideys. It was an article of faith with the Frontenacs that there was "always a breeze at Respide". She spoke of José. He was at Rabat, and had written to say that he was in no danger. All the same, she felt anxious, and would wake up in the night, worrying.

When the quarter of a hour was over, Yves kissed her again. She followed him out on to the landing. "I do hope they're careful, and don't drive too fast. I don't like to think of you rushing along the roads. Send me a wire this evening. . . ."

He took the stairs four at a time. When he reached the bottom, some instinct made him look up. Blanche Frontenac was leaning over the banisters. He saw the drawn face looking down at him.

"Only three weeks," he shouted.

"Yes, and do be careful."

And now, here he was in Bordeaux again on the way back. He would have liked to pay his mother a second surprise visit. But he could *not*, in the city of his birth, entertain these people at the *Chapon Fin*: they'd think he was trying to give them the slip. . . . Besides, Geo had said that he must be back in Paris that night, without fail. . . . He was feeling mad, because the young Englishman was sitting beside the girl, and he couldn't hear what they were saying. Their heads were close together. He could see them reflected in the windscreen. His remarks to Yves were scarcely encouraging: "I don't mind breaking my neck, so long as they break theirs too. . . ." Yves's reply had been: "Look out, there's a level-crossing coming."

He thought he might be able to get away after lunch. But he must wait for the bill. Geo, who was saying little and drinking a great deal, looked at his watch. "We shall be in Paris by seven. . . ." Until they reached the end of their journey his life would be in abeyance. He would be in torment until they reached Paris where he could get the girl to himself between the four walls of a room, and tell her, once and for all, that she wasn't to see that other chap again, that she had got to choose between them. . . . He was at the wheel of the car before Yves had settled up with the waiter. It would have been perfectly possible for Yves to say – "Give me just fifteen minutes," or even, "You go on without me: I'll come by train" – but it never occurred to him to do so. All he was concerned about was to fight down the inner compulsion which urged him to dash off and give his mother a kiss. 'It would be idiotic,' he told himself, 'to upset all their plans just to see her for five minutes, when in less than three weeks we shall be together again . . . I should barely have time to kiss her. . . .' A time was to come when he would never forgive himself for having grudged the few seconds needed in which to press his lips to a still living face. In some obscure region of himself he knew what the future held – for we are always warned. . . . While the women were in the cloak-room, he heard Geo say:

"Yves, do be a good fellow and sit in the back. I shan't feel so nervy with the Englishman beside me."

Yves replied that he himself would feel less nervy – and they set off. He found himself sandwiched between the two women. One of them said to the other:

"What, d'you mean to tell me that you haven't read *Paludes*? . . . it really is a scream . . . yes, Gide."

"I can't say I found it all that funny. . . . I remember now, I did read it. In what way is it funny?"

"I thought it a scream . . ."

"Yes, so you've said, but what is there so funny about it?"

"You explain what I mean, Frontenac."

"I haven't read it," he replied, as bold as brass.

"Not read *Paludes*?" – exclaimed the first speaker in tones of amazement.

"No, not read *Paludes*."

He was thinking of the staircase down which he had come three days earlier. He had glanced up. His mother had been looking over the banisters. 'I shall see her in a fortnight's time,' he thought. She would never know of his inconsiderateness in passing through Bordeaux without finding time to give her a kiss. At that moment he was more keenly aware of his love for her than he had ever been since the days of his young boyhood, when he had sobbed so bitterly on going back to school because of the thought that he would be separated from her each day until the evening. The two women were talking across him, though of whom he did not know.

"He begged me to get an invitation for him out of Marie-Constance. I told him I didn't know her well enough. He said, couldn't it be managed through Rose de Candale. I explained that I didn't want to run the risk of being snubbed for my pains, whereupon, my dear, believe it or not, he burst into tears. His whole future, his reputation, his very life, he said, was at stake. If he wasn't seen at that ball, he'd just have to fade out. I was foolish enough to observe that it was a very exclusive house. 'Exclusive!' he yelped: 'a house where *you're* invited!' "

"But, darling, it really is rather tragic for him. He's told everyone that he's going. The other day, at Ernesta's, I asked him, just for fun and to see how he'd carry it off, what he was going to be dressed as. 'As a slave-merchant,' he answered. The cheek of the man! – when, three days later, Ernesta and I, by agreement, asked him the same question, he said he wasn't at all sure that he was going, because he didn't find parties of that sort particularly amusing. . . ."

"Don't forget that I saw him cry – it really is too bad!"

"But that wasn't all. He went on to say that from what he could hear, Marie-Constance didn't mind whom she asked these days . . . and now that you've passed on what he said to you, I don't mind telling you, darling, that he quoted you as an instance. . . ."

"He's really rather a dangerous man, you know."

"He can start people gossiping. It doesn't matter how discredited a man may be. If he lunches, and dines, and sups out every day of the week, he's bound to be pretty formidable. He lays his eggs in the most likely spots . . . and then when they hatch out, and the little snakes go squirming all over the table-cloth, people don't know that he began it. . . ."

"Perhaps I'd *better* give Marie-Constance a ring this evening, what d'you think? After all, I *have* taken a thousand-franc box . . ."

"If only you can get him that invitation, he'll do anything in the world you want."

"There's nothing I want from him. . . ."

"All the same, you might ask him. . . ."

"What a little bitch you are, darling . . . you don't think, darling, not seriously? . . ."

"I'm not absolutely certain . . . but, after all, it'd only be a bit of what they call a *quid pro quo* . . ."

"A good deal more *quo* than *quid*. . . ."

"You really are a comic! . . . did you hear that, Frontenac?"

What was it his mother had said to him in the course of those five minutes? "There'll be masses of fruit at Respide. . . ."

A fine interchange of dirt was going on above his head between the painted mouths of the two women. He could have contributed to it without difficulty, but the filth which at any moment now might burst from him would belong only to the surface of his mind, and would have no place in those depths of his consciousness where, at this very moment, he could hear his mother saying: "There'll be masses of fruit this year". He could see her leaning over the banisters, watching him go downstairs, keeping him in sight until the last possible moment. The ghastly pallor of her face . . . "the pallor of heart-disease" – the words formed silently in his mind. . . . They came like a revealing flash. But even before he could catch and hold the omen, it had faded.

"Have it your own way . . . but what a fool the woman is! It's no good bores of her water trying to cling. You know as well as I do, that if she thought she could land somebody else, she wouldn't go about playing the poor, helpless little victim! She ought to be thankful that Alberto's put up with her for two whole years. I know he's taken his fun on the side, but even so it's beyond me how he's been patient with her for so long . . . and you know, don't you, that she's not nearly so rich as she led him to think?"

"But, when she starts talking about dying, it really does make one wonder. . . . Personally, I think there'll be a sticky end to it all. . . ."

"I wouldn't let that worry you. If the worst comes to the worst, she'll manage to wound herself just badly enough to get her husband into thoroughly bad odour. . . . You see if I'm not right! . . . She'll be on our backs for ever and ever, I bet! One can't *not* invite her, and if one thing's more certain than another it's that *she's* always free to accept!"

Yves thought about his mother's scruples in the matter of uncharitableness. . . . "I must remember to include that in my next confession" – she would say, when it happened that she had flared up at Burthe. . . . Jean-Louis's goodness of heart . . . his complete inability to smell out evil. . . . How miserable it made him when Yves laughed at Dussol! . . . The world, *this* world, in concert with which the last of the Frontenacs was howling at the top of his voice. . . . In Yves's eyes Jean-Louis's goodness was a counterbalance to the world's savagery. If he still believed in goodness, it was entirely owing to his mother and Jean-Louis. "I send you forth as lambs in the midst of wolves. . . ." Before him there rose on every side a vision of dark crowds with, in the midst of them, a quivering of veils and white coifs. . . . He, too, had been born to partake of this gentleness. He would go to Respide alone with his mother. Three weeks only stood between him and that time of torrid heat when there would be "masses of fruit". He would be careful not to wound her, would avoid giving her pain. This time he would know how not to get irritable. He made a silent promise that on the very first evening he would suggest that they should say their prayers together. She would not be able to believe her ears. He enjoyed in anticipation the joy that she would feel. He would confide in her . . . would, for instance, tell her what had happened to him in a night-club, on an evening of May. . . . It couldn't be helped, she'd got to know that he frequented such places. He would say: "I had drunk a little champagne . . . I was feeling sleepy, it was late. A woman stand-

ing on a table was singing a song. I was only half listening to
her. The people round about were joining in the chorus. It was
a soldiers' song, and everybody knew it. . . . In the middle of
the last verse, the name of Christ occurred, all mixed up with
a lot of filthy words. At that moment" (Yves had a vision of
his mother listening with that look upon her face of passionate
concentration . . . "at that moment I was conscious of a feeling
of pain, of almost physical pain, as though the blasphemy had
struck straight to my heart." She would get up from her chair,
would give him a kiss, would say something like – "You
see, darling, how grace . . ." He could imagine the night,
the swarm of stars in the August sky, the smell of the late
crops coming from the mill which would be invisible in the
darkness. . . .

During the days that followed he felt reassured. Nothing had
happened. Never had he lived so dissipated an existence. It was
the time of year when, before the general exodus of summer,
those who live for pleasure cram more and more of it into their
mouths: the time when those who love suffer agonies at the
thought of inevitable separation, and when those who are loved
can at last breathe freely: the time when the burned-up chest-
nuts of the Paris streets see, at dawn, gathered round stationary
cars, men in evening dress, and women shivering in the night
air, all drawing out their last farewells, so as to keep, as long
as possible, from the necessity of parting.

On one such night it so happened that Yves had not gone
out. Perhaps he was feeling lazy, perhaps he was ill, perhaps he
was suffering from heart-ache. Whatever the reason, he was
alone in his small room, suffering from his solitude, as only at
that age can one suffer, when solitude seems of all ills the most
intolerable, the one from which at all costs, one must escape.
His whole existence was so organized that there should never

be an evening unfilled. But on this occasion the machinery had broken down. We manipulate others as though they were pawns: we are careful to see that no square upon the board shall be empty. But they, too, play their secret game, pushing us about as the fancy takes them, brushing us aside, so that we feel ourselves laid by, snuffed, extinguished. The voice which, at the very last moment, says on the telephone – "I'm terribly sorry, but I just can't make it," is always the voice belonging to the one of any given couple who need make no excuses, who can follow the whim of the moment. Had Yves's loneliness, on that particular evening, not been due to the absence of a certain woman, he could have dressed, gone out, and hunted up his friends. If he sat motionless, without a light, it was, no doubt, because he had received a terrible blow and was silently bleeding in the darkness.

The telephone rang, but not with its accustomed sound. The trills were rapid and urgent. He heard a lot of "crackling" – then: "Bordeaux's calling you." He thought at first that it must be his mother, and that she was ill. But before he had had time to feel the possibility as pain, a voice, which was indeed his mother's, came through, very faint, and as though speaking from another world. She belonged to the generation which has never learned how to master the telephone.

"Is that you, Yves: mamma speaking."

"I can hardly hear you."

He gathered that she had had an acute attack of rheumatism, that she was being packed off to Dax, and that her arrival at Respide would be delayed for ten days.

"I hope you can join me at Dax, so that we shan't lose any of our time together."

It was to get that promise from him that she had telephoned. He replied that he would join her as soon as she liked. She could not hear him. He repeated what he had said, grew impatient.

"Yes, mamma, I'll come to Dax."

From very far away the poor old voice kept saying the same thing over and over again. "You'll come to Dax, then?" Suddenly, the line went dead. For a while he did all he could to re-establish the connexion, but without success. He remained where he was, not moving from his chair. He felt miserable.

By next day the whole incident had passed from his mind. He resumed his normal existence, enjoying himself, or, rather, pursuing until dawn, the flittings of a woman who was enjoying *herself*. He did not get home until the small hours, and slept late. One morning, the sound of the door-bell woke him. He thought it must be the postman with a registered letter. He pushed the door ajar, and saw Jean-Louis. He took him into the sitting-room and opened the shutters. A yellow fog lay upon the roof-tops. Without looking at Jean-Louis he asked whether he had come to Paris on business. The answer was more or less what he had expected: their mother was not at all well, and Jean-Louis had looked up Yves with the intention of urging him to make an earlier start for the country. Yves looked at his brother. He was wearing a grey suit and a black tie with white dots. He asked why he hadn't been wired for, or rung up on the telephone.

"I didn't want to frighten you by sending a telegram, and it's always so difficult to explain things on the telephone."

"Maybe – but that's no reason for leaving mamma. I'm amazed that you should come away, even for twenty-four hours. Why *have* you come? . . ."

Jean-Louis looked at him fixedly. Yves, rather pale, asked quietly:

"Is she dead?"

Jean-Louis took his hand: his eyes never left his face.

Yves murmured: "I knew it."

"How could you have known?"

He said again, "I – knew it," while his brother hastily embarked upon the details which Yves had not, as yet, thought to demand.

"It was Monday night, no, Tuesday, that she began complaining for the first time. . . ."

It surprised him, all the time he was speaking, to see how calmly Yves had taken the news. He felt disappointed. He might just as well have spared himself the journey, might have stayed beside his mother's body while it was still there, and not lost one of those last, sad moments. He could not guess that a scruple in Yves's mind was "drawing" his sorrow to a point, like one of those abscesses which a doctor deliberately provokes. . . . Had his mother known that he had passed through Bordeaux without troubling to go to see her? Had the knowledge caused her pain? Was he a monster not to have made the effort? If he had spent a few moments with her on his way back from Guéthary, they would probably have been nothing but a repetition of their meeting on his way there—a few pieces of advice, a few requests that he should be careful, a kiss. She would have followed him out on to the landing, would have leaned over the banisters, would have watched him down the stairs for as long as she could see him. Anyhow, if he hadn't visited her again, he had at least heard her voice on the telephone. He had caught everything she had said, though she, poor woman, had had difficulty in hearing his replies. . . . He asked Jean-Louis whether she had had time to mention him. No, she had been expecting to see her "Parisian" so soon again, that her mind had been preoccupied with José, who was still in Morocco. At length Yves's tears began to flow, and Jean-Louis was conscious of a feeling of relief. His own attitude was one of complete calm. He refused to let himself brood upon his

sorrow. He looked round the room in which yesterday's un-
tidiness had not yet been cleared away. The Russian "craze" of
the last few years was evidenced by the colours of divan and
cushions. But the man who lived here, thought Jean-Louis, had
probably taken only a passing pleasure in them. He would have
said at a guess that his brother was indifferent to such things. . . .
For a few moments Jean-Louis was guilty of disloyalty to his
mother who was dead, in the interest of his brother who was
alive. He gave his mind entirely to the scene about him, trying
to discover signs and traces. . . . There was one photograph,
and one only – of Nijinski, in the *Spectre de la Rose*. Jean-Louis
stared at his brother standing there with his back to the fire-
place. He looked so frail in his blue pyjamas, with his hair all
anyhow. His face, now that he was crying, was just as it used
to be when he was a little boy. Very quietly, Jean-Louis told
him to get dressed. Left to himself, he seemed to be putting a
silent question to the walls, to the cigarette ash on the table,
to the burn in the carpet.

XVI

ALL that the parish could muster in the way of priests and
choir-boys walked ahead of the hearse. Yves, who was
with his two brothers and Uncle Xavier, was keenly
aware of the ridiculous picture they must make in the garish
daylight with their woebegone faces, and how absurd his evening clothes and silk hat must look (José was wearing the
uniform of the Colonial Infantry). He observed the expressions
of the people standing on the sidewalk, the eager, hungry

curiosity in the women's eyes. He did not feel particularly miserable, did not, indeed, feel anything at all. He could hear snatches of what Uncle Alfred and Dussol were saying behind him ("you must follow immediately behind us" – the latter had been told: "after all, you're one of the family.")

"She was a woman with a head on her shoulders," Dussol was saying: "and I know no greater compliment than that. I would even go so far as to say that she was a true business-woman – or, rather, that she would have become one if she had had a husband at her side to train her up."

"In business," Caussade remarked, "women can do a lot of things that we can't."

"D'you remember how she behaved at the time of the Métairie affair, Caussade? – that lawyer chap who did a bunk. He got away with sixty thousand francs of hers. She knocked me up at midnight. She was on her way to see Madame Métairie, and wanted me to go with her. Blanche made her hand over a written acknowledgement of all the money owing. That wasn't an easy job, I can tell you: it needed pluck. . . . The legal proceedings dragged on for ten years, but she got every penny, in the long run, and before any of the other creditors, too. That's what I call a nice piece of work!"

"Yes, but I've often heard her say that if it hadn't been for the children, whose trustee she was, she'd never have had the courage to go on."

"That's very likely, because at times she was scrupulous to excess – it was her only weakness. . . ."

Uncle Alfred, with a sanctimonious air, protested that that had been her most admirable characteristic.

Dussol gave a shrug.

"You must forgive me for smiling! I'm an honest man, as men go, and our firm is generally looked upon as an example of everything that's above board. . . . But you and I know what business is. Blanche would have agreed with me. . . . She loved money, you know, and wasn't ashamed of loving it."

"She preferred land."

"But not for its own sake. In her eyes, land stood for wealth. She thought of it in the same way as she thought of bank-notes, the only difference being that she considered it safer. She often told me that, taking one year with another, and allowing for overheads, she reckoned that her landed property brought her in regularly between four and a half and five per cent."

Yves conjured up a picture of his mother as she had looked, sitting at nightfall on the terrace, among the Bourideys pines. Again, he could see her, in imagination, coming towards him along the path that made the circuit of the park, with her Rosary in her hand. He thought of her, too, at Respide, speaking of God beneath the slumbering hills. He searched his memory for things she had said which bore witness to her love of the land. Jean-Louis had told him how, just before she died, she had pointed through the open window at the June sky and the bird-infested trees, and said: "That's what I really regret."

"I'm told" – said Dussol – "that her last words were about the vines. She pointed to them and said: 'How I regret that I shan't be there to see the wonderful harvest!' . . ."

"That's not what I heard. I was led to suppose that she was referring to the countryside in general, and the beauties of nature. . . ."

"That's what her sons say" (Dussol lowered his voice) "but they, of course, interpreted her words in their own way: you know what they're like. . . . Poor Jean-Louis! . . . I prefer my version. It seems to me far more beautiful. I like to think that what she was mourning was the crop that she would never gather, the fruit of the vineyards which she had been at such pains to renew. . . . Nothing will make me believe differently. I knew her for forty years. Once, when she was complaining of her sons, I told her that she was a hen that had hatched out a brood of ducklings . . . how she laughed!"

"No, Dussol, no: she was proud of them, and rightly so!"

"I don't deny it. But I can't help laughing when Jean-Louis insists that she had a liking for all the stuff that Yves produces. Intelligence was her outstanding quality. She was a very model of the normal, good-sense incarnate, and I know what I'm talking about! At the time when I was having all those difficulties with Jean-Louis over his precious profit-sharing schemes and boring social theories, I felt in my bones that she was on my side. She was worried about what she called his 'day-dreaming'. She begged me not to let it influence my opinion of him. 'Give him time' – she used to say. 'You'll see he's got his head screwed on the right way, really.' "

Yves had forgotten all about his ridiculous clothes and patent-leather shoes. He was no longer studying the faces of the people on the sidewalk. Imprisoned in the procession which stretched from the hearse to Dussol (a single word, caught by chance, was enough to tell him all that the man was saying), he moved, with his eyes upon the ground. 'She loved the poor,' he was thinking. 'When we were small she took us into all the slum rooms when she went visiting. Her heart went out to girls in trouble, if only they repented of their ways. She could never read without crying the memories of childhood that found their way into my poems. . . .'

Dussol's voice was droning on and on: "Dealers had to watch their step with her. I've never known anyone with such an eye for accounts, nor anyone who could cut down percentages as she could."

"Did you ever listen to her talking things over with any of her tenants, Dussol? Somehow she always managed to make them pay for their own repairs."

Yves knew from Jean-Louis that this was not true; that leases had been renewed in the most reckless way imaginable, and quite irrespective of enhanced values. All the same, he could not dismiss from his mind the caricature of his mother, as she appeared to other people, stripped of the Frontenac mystery, which Dussol's words had built up. Death condemns us to be the prey not of worms only but of men. They nibble away at remembered lives until there is nothing left of them. Already, Yves, under the influence of this overheard conversation, found himself no longer seeing the dead woman as he had known her. Her flesh had outlived corruption longer than her reputation. It was essential that he should reconstruct his memory of her, and wipe away these alien stains. Blanche Frontenac must again become for him what she had always been. Only if she did, could he go on living, could he survive her. How endless seemed the walk to the cemetery down the long rue d'Arès, past slum dwellings and brothels, with the Family trailing along in dress clothes and shiny shoes – all this grotesque barbarism of funeral pomp, and the hurried muttering of the sublime Office of the Church by priests who, as the saying goes, were "practised" in it – only, too, too practised! Dussol had kept his voice low, but now he raised it again, and Yves could not resist the temptation to listen.

"No, Caussade, I can't agree with you there. She was an admirable woman, but there, I think, she failed. The bringing up of the young was not her strong point. . . . I am not, myself, without a certain feeling for religion. The parish clergy will always find me ready to listen if they think I can help them in their difficulties. They know that, and the knowledge is of some value to them. But if I had had sons I should have seen to it that, once the First Communion was over, they should have turned to and prepared themselves for the serious business of life. Blanche never really took into account the weight of heredity that lay upon her boys. I don't want to speak evil of poor Michel Frontenac . . ."

Caussade protested that Michel had been a professed anticlerical all his life, but Dussol went on:

"That's as may be, but it doesn't alter the fact that he was a dreamer, the kind of man who will go to a Board Meeting with a book stuffed away in his pocket. That'll show you the sort of chap he was. Why, I've even seen him bring a volume of poetry into the office when there was a sales conference on! Once, when that happened, I picked it up, but he snatched it from me in a shamefaced sort of way. . . ."

"Shamefaced? – why? – was it what's usually called a 'curious' book?"

"Oh, dear me no! He didn't go in for *that* kind of thing – on second thoughts, though, you mayn't be so far out . . . I remember, now, it was one of Baudelaire's . . . *La Charogne* . . . know it? . . . A sensitive soul was Michel, but no good at all when it came to business, and, mind you, I was pretty well placed to judge. It was a good thing for the firm and for the Frontenac children that I was there. Blanche's religious fervour did go some way to developing certain tendencies in *them*, and, well . . . you've only got to look around to see what the results have been. . . ."

Once more, he lowered his voice. Yves repeated to himself those last few words – 'what the results have been'. Could he truthfully be called a man? Yes, but not what Dussol meant by a man. But what, if it came to that, did Dussol mean by a man? And what could Blanche Frontenac have done to make her sons different from what they had become? After all, Jean-Louis had, as they say, founded a family, and was showing himself to be pretty efficient in the business. His influence was a good deal more considerable than Dussol's, and his reputation as a "socially conscious" employer, had spread far and wide.

José was risking his life in Morocco (no, that wasn't quite true: he hadn't stirred from Rabat): and Yves . . . well, at least they must know that he was always being talked about in the papers. . . . In what way were the Frontenac boys different from other boys? . . . To that question he would have found it difficult to find an answer. . . . All the same, that damned Dussol, teetering along behind him like a moving mountain of flesh, still had the power to reduce him to a state of pure gibber, to humiliate him till it hurt.

Standing on the brink of the open grave, in the little knot of "real friends" ("I made a particular point of going with her to the very end"), Yves, his eyes dim with tears, his ears deaf to everything, did, nevertheless, manage to hear, above the rattle of stones on the coffin, and the heavy breathing of the grave-diggers – who looked, for all the world, like stage murderers, – the self-satisfied, the implacable voice of Dussol:

"She was a thoroughly capable woman."

That day, as a mark of respect for the dead woman, no work was done at Respide or at Bourideys. The oxen stayed in the byre, and thought it must be Sunday. The men went to the inn and sat drinking in an atmosphere of anise. A storm was blowing up, and Burthe feared for the hay. How put about the poor lady would have been if she had known that, because of her, it hadn't been got under cover! The Hure flowed on beneath the alders. Close to the old oak, just where the wall had been knocked down, the moon struck a sparkle in the grass from the sacred medal which Blanche had lost three years before, during the Easter holidays, and which the children had long looked for and never found.

XVII

ALL through the following winter, and the early months of 1913, Yves's mood seemed to be more bitter than ever before. He was beginning to lose his hair; his cheeks were sunken; there was a feverish glitter in his eyes, and the bony structure of his brow had become more than usually prominent. All the same, he felt deeply shocked at the ease with which he had become resigned to his loss. He did not really miss his mother at all. Since, for a long time now, he had been living away from her, nothing was altered in the routine of his days, and he would go for weeks together without once thinking of her. The only difference in him was that he had come to demand more of the people he was fond of. The craving to be loved, which his mother had never failed to satisfy, he now centred on others who, though up till now, they might have filled his thoughts, made him restless, and even occasioned him some little suffering, had never really torn his life up by the roots. He had been accustomed to plunge into his mother's love as he had plunged into the park at Bourideys. It led straight into the pine-forest, and, as a child, he had always known that he could walk on and on, night and day, and that in the end he would reach the sea. Into every love he now wormed his way, moved by a fatal curiosity, seeking to find its limits, yet always obscurely hoping that he would never come on them. Alas! a very few steps brought him there, all the more surely because his mania was turning him into a wearisome and insupportable companion. He was for ever demonstrating to the women of his choice that their fondness for him was only a seeming passion. He belonged to that unhappy race of young men who go on, again and again, saying – "You don't love

144

me!" in the hope of getting an assurance to the contrary. But his words had more power to convince than he realized, so that to her who ventured on a mild protest, he would himself give proofs so unanswerable that he ended by convincing her of the truth – that she did not love him, nor ever had done.

In that spring of 1913, he had reached the point at which his sufferings had become like one of those physical ailments for the end of which the patient eagerly watches, hour by hour, in terror at the thought that he may not be able to endure it a moment longer. Even at parties, if the object of his passion happened to be present, he was quite incapable of hiding his wound, but displayed his suffering for all to see, and left a trail of blood wherever he went.

He was quite convinced that he was the prey to an obsession. He found himself continually harking back to instances of treachery which had existed only in his imagination, so that he could never be quite sure, even when he caught his mistress in the act, that he had not been misled by hallucination. If she gave him her solemn word that it had not been her he had seen in a car beside the young man with whom she had been dancing on the previous evening, he allowed himself to be convinced, even though he felt quite certain that he had recognized her. . . . 'I am going mad,' he said to himself, and chose deliberately to believe that he was indeed mad, in the first place, because it would give him some sort of breathing-space, however short, between bouts of suffering, and because he could see in the face he loved a look of unfeigned alarm. "You *must* believe me," she would insist, moved by a fierce longing to console and reassure him. Against this form of hypnotism he was never proof. "Look me in the eyes: *now* do you believe me?"

It wasn't that she was better than anybody else, but he always failed to realize, until it was too late, that he had the

power to awaken a sort of patient tenderness in those who, in
other ways, were the source of his torment. It was as though,
when they were with him, they all unknowingly became
saturated with that maternal love the warmth of which
had swaddled him for so many years. In August, the earth,
impregnated by the sun, retains its warmth until late into
the night. And so it was that the love of his dead mother was
still about him, softening the hardest hearts.

It was that, perhaps, which kept him from succumbing to
the blows that rained upon him. For there was no other support
on which he could lean, and he could expect no help from his
family. What remained of the Frontenac mystery came to him
now only in the form of scattered fragments from a complete
and utter wreck. The first time he went back to Bourideys
after his mother's death, he felt as though he were walking in
a dream, as though he were moving through a past now suddenly materialized. He brooded over the pines rather than saw
them. He remembered the secret flow of waters under the
alder trees. The ones he looked at were lopped: the new shoots
were already intertwined. But he substituted for them in his
mind the moss-grown trunks which once, in earlier holidays,
the Hure had mirrored. The smell from the meadows worried
him because there was more in it of mint than he remembered.
He felt himself as much cluttered by the house and park as by
his mother's old umbrellas, and those garden hats they could
not give away, and would not jettison (there was one very old
one embroidered with swallows). A whole section of the
Frontenac mystery had, as it were, been sucked into that spot
as into a hole in the ground, a cavern in which the mother of
Jean-Louis and José, of Yves, of Danièle and Marie Frontenac,
had been laid to rest. When, on occasion, a face looked out
from a world now three parts destroyed, the effect on Yves was
one of nightmare.

One fine morning, in the summer of 1913, he saw, framed
in the doorway of his room, a large woman whom he recognized at once, though he had seen her only once before, and
then, casually, in the street. The truth was that Joséfa had, for
many years, been a constant joke in the Frontenac family.
Could it be that he didn't know who she was? Monsieur Yves
must surely have been aware of her existence? The young men
of the family must always have realized that their uncle did not
live alone? Poor man, he had always been at such pains to keep
her existence from them, and the knowledge that that was so
made her feel awful! . . . But perhaps it was just as well that
things had turned out like this. He had recently had two bad
attacks of angina at her place (he must be in a bad way, otherwise she would never have had the courage to call on Yves).
The doctor had utterly pooh-poohed the idea of his going
home, and now the poor dear was worrying himself sick, night
and day, at the idea that he might die without ever seeing his
nephews again. But now they knew that there had been a
woman in their uncle's life, so what point could there be in
trying to keep it secret any longer? . . . Nevertheless he would
have to be prepared for the revelation, because he had no idea
that his wrong-doing had been discovered. . . . She would tell
him that the family had only quite recently tumbled to the
truth, and that they had forgiven him. . . . Yves remarked,
drily, that it was not for the young Frontenacs to "forgive" a
man whom they respected more than anybody else in the
world. The large woman, however, stuck to her point.

"You see, Monsieur Yves – and I can say this to you now
that you are of an age to know what's what – there has been
nothing between us for years . . . after all, we're neither of us
exactly young . . . besides, I couldn't dream of allowing the
poor man to go a-wearing of himself out, and him in such a
condition, too. I never could forgive myself if I thought I'd had

a hand in killing him. . . . He's more like my child than anything else, and a very young child too. . . . I am not the kind
of person you take me for . . . might very naturally take me
for. . . . You can ask the parish clergy, if you like: *they* know
all about me!"

She spoke mincingly, as they had always imagined she
would. She was wearing a Russian-ballet coat with loose
sleeves, secured at the waist by a single button. Her eyes still
showed as handsome under the cloche hat which did nothing
to conceal the thick, tip-tilted nose, the vulgar mouth, the
retreating chin. She looked at "Monsieur Yves" with deep
emotion. Though she had never met the Frontenac children,
she had been familiar with them from their youth up. She had
followed their progress through life, step by step, and had
taken an interest in all their childish ailments. Nothing was
insignificant to her that occurred in the glorious empyrean of
the Frontenacs. Far, far above her, they moved as demi-gods,
whose smallest gestures she could, by an extraordinary piece of
luck, follow from the deep abyss of her own existence . . . and
though in the wonderful world of fantasy in which her day-
dreams moved, she had often imagined herself as married to
Xavier, and participating in moving scenes of family affection,
with Blanche calling her "sister", and the children, "Aunt
Joséfa", she had never really thought that anything remotely
resembling this meeting could ever occur, or that the day
would come when she would find herself face to face with one
of the young Frontenacs, and speak with him as with an equal.

Yet so vivid was her feeling of having known Yves always,
that now, face to face with this lean and melancholy man
whom she was seeing for the first time, she found herself
thinking 'how thin he has grown!'

"And how is Monsieur José? – still enjoying himself in
Morocco? Your uncle is terribly anxious about him. It seems

as things over there are beginning to hum, and the papers don't tell you everything by a long chalk! What a good thing it is that your poor dear mother is not here, for she would be worrying herself to a shadow!"

Yves asked her to sit down, but himself remained standing. He made a valiant effort to struggle to the surface of his emotional preoccupations, to seem at least to be listening and taking an interest. To himself he said: 'Uncle Xavier is very ill: Uncle Xavier is going to die. He is the last of the older generation of Frontenacs. . . .' But he lashed at his feelings to no avail. It was impossible for him to feel anything but the frightful threat hanging over his head, the threat of the summer's end, of the weeks and months of separation, weeks and months that would be heavy with storms, beaten by furious rains, burned by devastating suns. The whole of creation, with its stars in their courses and its mortal scourges would soon be rearing itself between him and the object of his passion. When next he found himself close to her it would be autumn. Till then he must fight his way in solitude through an ocean of flame.

It had been arranged that he should spend his holidays with Jean-Louis, in that home which his mother had so ardently desired should be a refuge for him when she was no more. To this necessity he might have resigned himself if only the pain of parting had been shared. But "she" was to go for a long cruise on a yacht. "She" was living in a fever of "tryings-on", and made no attempt to conceal her excitement. Anticipated pleasure shone in her eyes. Nor, for him, was it a matter of imaginary suspicions, of fears now awakened, now allayed. What he had to face was something far worse – the cruel happiness, more murderous than any treachery, felt by a young woman at the prospect of getting away from him. What made her drunk was killing him. With endless patience she had made pretence of tenderness and loyalty. But now, suddenly, she had torn the mask from her face, though not deliberately nor with joy, because she had no wish to cause him pain.

"It's the best thing that could have happened. You know perfectly well that I am bad for you. . . . By October you'll be completely cured. . . ."

"But there was a time when you said you hoped I never should be cured."

"When did I say that? I don't remember."

"Last January: one Tuesday. We were just leaving Fischer's. We passed the *Gagne-Petit*, and you looked at yourself in the window."

She shook her head. She seemed annoyed. Those words of hers had struck sweet music to his heart. For weeks he had lived on them, repeating them over and over to himself, long after their power to charm had vanished. And now, here she was, denying that she had ever spoken them! . . . It was all his fault. He so enlarged the smallest things she said. He had grown into such a habit of giving them a fixed value, an unalterable significance, and, half the time, they expressed nothing but a moment's mood.

"Are you sure I said that? I may have done, it's just that I don't remember."

It was only yesterday evening that Yves had heard that terrible comment. It had been made here between these very same walls where now there sat a fat, fair woman who was giving evidence of heat, heat so extreme that it was difficult to sit in the same room with her, even with the window open. Joséfa seemed now to be thoroughly settled in. Her eyes were fixed, with absorbed attention, on Yves.

"And Monsieur Jean-Louis? – what a splendid young man he is! – and Madame Jean-Louis, such a distinguished-looking lady. That photograph of them together, taken at Coutenceau's with the baby between them, stands on your uncle's desk. Such a sweet little girl! Anyone would know from her mouth and chin that she's a Frontenac! Often's the time I've said to your uncle, 'She's the very spit and image of a Frontenac!' He loves children, even quite tiny ones. . . . When my daughter, the one as lives at Niort and is married to a very solid fellow in the wholesale (and he has to shoulder all the responsibility along of his boss suffering from the rheumatism in his joints) . . . when my daughter brought her baby to see me, he took her on his knee, and my daughter passed the remark as it was easy to see that he was used to children. . . ."

She broke off, suddenly overcome by shyness. Monsieur Yves wasn't being exactly forthcoming. Most probably he took her for a scheming woman. . . .

"I think you ought to know how things are, Monsieur Yves. . . . He gave me a lump sum down, once and for all, and the furniture. . . . It's all there. I wouldn't like to be thought one as could do the least little thing to hurt the family. . . ."

She spoke of "the family" as though no other family existed in the world. To Yves's consternation two tears, as large as lentils, began to trickle down her face. The Frontenacs, he protested, had never suspected her of the slightest impropriety. On the contrary, they felt deeply grateful for the way in which she had looked after their uncle. In his anxiety to treat her with proper consideration, he ignored the claims of common caution, and overshot the mark. She broke down entirely, and her trickle of tears became a flood.

"I do love him so! . . . I do love him so!" she spluttered, "and all of you as well, though to be sure I always knew as I wasn't good enough even to speak to you, but I've always loved every member of the family, as my daughter at Niort can witness to, she having often reproached me for it and complaining that I'm more interested in the Frontenac children than in my own flesh and blood, which it's true. . . ."

Her face was streaming, and she began feeling about in her bag for a clean handkerchief. At that moment, the telephone rang.

"Hullo . . . Oh, it's you . . . dinner? . . . half a moment while I look at my book. . . ."

Yves held the receiver away from his ear for a moment. Joséfa, who was sniffing and watching him closely, was surprised to see that he did not, in fact, look at his engagement book at all, but stared before him with an expression of blissful happiness.

"Yes, I can manage it with a little juggling. . . . It's sweet of you to spare me one more evening. . . . Where? . . . the *Pré Catalan*? . . . Shall I pick you up? . . . but it would be so easy for me . . . why not? . . . what's that? . . . I'm not making a point of anything . . . it's only that I might be a bit late and don't want you to have to hang about alone at the restaurant. . . . I said, I don't want you to have to hang about . . . what's that? . . . you won't be alone? . . . Who's the other? . . . Geo? . . . No, of course I don't mind. . . . I'm not in the least annoyed . . . what? . . . well, of course it won't be the same thing . . . I said, of course it won't be the same thing. . . . I'm not being difficult. . . ."

Joséfa was devouring him with her eyes. Like an old circus horse roused by the sound of distant music, she snuffed the air and pawed the ground. Yves had hung up the receiver, and the face he turned to her was drawn with pain. She did not realize that he was with difficulty keeping himself from showing her to the door, though it did occur to her that the time had come to make a move. He would write to Jean-Louis, he said, about their uncle. As soon as he heard, he would get into touch with her. An endless fumbling ensued while she tried to find a card with her address. At long last, she went.

Uncle Xavier is very ill; Uncle Xavier is dying – Yves spoke the words over and over to himself. He tried to call up visual images to make him realize their import; Uncle Xavier sitting in a big armchair in the gloomy rue de Cursol house, under the shadow of the great parental bed . . . himself, holding out his cheek to be kissed, and his uncle breaking off his reading with a "run along, my chick" . . . his uncle in a city suit, standing on the bank of the Hure, and carving a piece of pine-bark into the shape of a boat . . . *Sabe, sabe, caloumet, te pourterey un pan naouet* . . . But in vain did he cast his net, in vain draw it in filled with a swarm of wriggling memories. One and all, they slipped free and fell back. Those pictures of the past were scrawled over now with larger and more recent figures – the figures of that hateful woman and her Geo. What business had Geo to come butting in? – and why tonight of all nights? It was their last chance of being together. Must Geo come too? . . . Why had she gone out of her way to pick on him, and not on somebody else . . . why this man, who was his friend, of whom he had grown fond? . . . There had been a calculated note of surprise in her voice. She did not want to seem to be concealing the fact that she and Geo had struck up an intimacy. . . . He, too, must almost certainly be going away somewhere this summer, though where, Yves had not succeeded in finding out. Oh God! – *of course*, he was to be one of the yacht party. Geo and she, for weeks and weeks, on the deck, in the cabins – she and Geo . . .

He flung himself face downwards on the divan, and worried the back of his hand with his teeth. This was more than he could bear: this time he *would* get his own back on that bitch of a woman, would really do something that would hurt her! But how could he manage to throw mud without some of it sticking to himself? . . . He'd find *some* way. . . . He'd put her into a book, so's she'd be bound to be recognized! He would conceal nothing! he would smother her with filth! She should appear in his pages as someone at once grotesque and loath-some. . . . All her little secret habits, all her physical peculiari-ties, should be writ large. . . . But it would take time to get it written . . . much easier, much quicker just to kill her. He could do that this very evening, now, at once. He'd see to it that she was given time enough to realize what was coming to her, time in which to be afraid – she, who was such a coward! She must see herself dying, mustn't die at once, must realize that she had been disfigured. . . .

Slowly the hatred drained from him. He pressed out the last drop. Then, very gently, and in a low voice, he uttered the name he loved so well. Again and again he murmured it, dwelling on each syllable. It was all of her that he could have. No one in the world could stop him from whispering that name, from crying it aloud. But upstairs were the neighbours, who would hear every sound. At Bourideys he could have taken refuge in his little hide-out. By now the bracken must have grown over the tiny arena where once, on an autumn day, long years ago, the future had been revealed to him. In imagina-tion he could see that small, that scarcely perceptible point on the earth's surface, filled with the drone of wasps in the hot morning sunshine. The pale heather would be sweet with the smell of honey, and a light breeze, perhaps, would be drifting down a mist of pollen from the tall pines. He could see, in its every detail, the path that led back to the house under the branchy shadows of the park – could see the exact spot where once he had met his mother. Over her party dress she had thrown the little violet shawl which had come from Salies. She had put it round his shoulders because she had felt him shiver.

"Mamma!" – he groaned: "Mamma!"

He lay there sobbing. He was the first of all the Frontenac

brothers to call upon their dead mother as though she were living still. Eighteen months later it was to be the turn of José, lying with a hole in his belly, through an interminable September night, between the trenches.

XVIII

AS soon as she got into the street, Joséfa's thoughts went back to her patient. He was quite alone, and at any moment he might have an attack. She regretted the long time she had spent with Yves, and reproached herself bitterly. But so well had she been trained by Xavier that it never so much as occurred to her to take a taxi. She hurried towards the rue de Sèvres, where she could catch the Saint-Sulpice-Auteuil tram. She walked, as she always did, with her stomach well forward, and her nose in the air, muttering to herself, much to the delight of the passers-by, the words "Hé-bé!" in an angry, outraged voice. She was thinking of Yves, and now that the young man was no longer there to fascinate and dazzle her with his physical presence, her thoughts were bitter. How little he had seemed to care when she had told him of his uncle's illness! At the very moment when the poor man was drawing near his end, terrified at the thought that he might not be able to say good-bye to his nephews, the young man had been busy tele- phoning to some countess or other (Joséfa had caught sight of the cards stuck in the frame of Yves's mirror – *Baron et Baronne de . . . Marquise de . . . The English Ambassador, and Lady . . .*) This evening he would be dining to the sound of music with one of those great ladies . . . terrible hussies they were, too . . . she'd read all about *them* in that serial of Charles

Mérouvel's . . . and *he* knew what he was writing about, none better!

These hostile sentiments covered a deep-seated pain. For the first time Joséfa was realizing the simple-mindedness of the poor old fellow who had sacrificed everything to an empty dream of pulling the wool over his nephews' eyes. He had always been so ashamed of the life he was leading – a remarkably innocent life, really! His career of gilded vice had been such a very mild affair! The two of them, he and she, had gone without, and all for the sake of a pack of young fellows who would never know what he had sacrificed for them, and would have laughed if they had been told. . . . She climbed into the tram-car, and sat wiping her purple face. . . . She still suffered from rushes of blood to the head, though less than last year. Pray heaven, nothing had happened to Xavier! It was really very convenient having a tram-stop just in front of the house.

She climbed the four flights of stairs, puffing and blowing. Xavier was sitting in the dining-room, close to the half-open window. He was panting slightly, and was quite motionless. He said that he was suffering scarcely any pain, and that it was marvellous to be without it. He was perfectly all right so long as he did not move. He felt a bit peckish, but would rather go without food than run the risk of an attack. The Metro bridge was almost level with the window, and almost every minute a train went clanging and banging by. It never occurred either to Xavier or to Joséfa to be worried by the noise. They lived hedged in by the pieces of furniture from Angoulême which were far too big for the tiny rooms. The cupid's torch had been badly chipped during the move, and several of the ornaments on the wardrobe had come unstuck.

She soaked some "fingers" of bread and butter in a soft-boiled egg, and tried to get the old man to eat. She spoke to him as she might have done to a child: "Come along, ducky:

come along, my pet . . ." He did not move so much as a
muscle. He was like one of those insects who find in immobility
their sole means of defence. Towards evening, in the sudden
silence between trains, he heard the swifts crying, as once they
had cried in the garden at Preignac.

All of a sudden, he spoke:

"I shan't see the children again."

"Time enough later on to think about that . . . though if it
would make your mind any easier, I've only to send them a
telegram. . . ."

"That will have to wait until the doctor lets me go home. . . ."

"Why shouldn't they come and see you here? You can
always say you've moved, and that I'm your housekeeper."

He seemed to hesitate a moment, then shook his head.

"They would see at once that the furniture isn't mine . . .
and even if they didn't find out, they couldn't possibly come
to a place like this. Even if they never knew, I couldn't let
them come here, for the family's sake."

"You talk as though I'd got the plague!" She was up in arms.
Never, while Xavier was in health, had she uttered a word of
complaint, but now that he was at death's door, she spoke out.
He sat quite still, careful not to make the slightest movement.

"You're a good soul . . . but for the sake of Michel's memory
his sons must never . . . It's not a question of you, but of
principle. . . . Besides, how wretched it would be, after success-
fully keeping it dark for so long . . ."

"Oh come now: surely you can't believe that they haven't
known about it for ages?"

She regretted her outburst when she saw him move uneasily
in his chair, and heard his quickened breathing.

"No, I don't mean that. Of course they don't know a thing.
What I meant was that, even if they did, they wouldn't hold it
against you."

"Oh, I know they are too good-hearted ever to dream of criticizing me, still . . ."

Joséfa moved away from his chair, and leaned out of the window. . . . Good-hearted, indeed! She thought of Yves as she had seen him that morning, at the telephone, pretending to consult his engagement-book, with an expression on his face that was half bewilderment, half happiness. She imagined him now, at this moment, in what she called his "fish-tails", and his "crush-hat", in one of those grand restaurants where there is a little pink-shaded lamp on each table. Trains packed full of men going home after the day's work, were rattling across the iron bridge. Xavier seemed rather more breathless than he had been during the afternoon. He explained by signs that he did not wish to speak, to be spoken to, or to eat. It was as though he were rolling himself into a ball, aping death in order to escape from death's reality. Night fell, warm and close. The window was left open in spite of the doctor's orders. He had told her to shut it, because, when an angina patient, he said, has one of his attacks, he doesn't know what he is doing. . . . Joséfa thought of the world's misery. . . . She was sitting between the window and the sick man's chair. She felt oppressed by the large pieces of furniture which once had been her pride. This evening, suddenly, she saw them as mean and wretched. . . . No more workmen, now. The trains going towards the Etoile were almost empty. That's where one changes for the Porte Dauphine. Joséfa had often got out there with Xavier, squeezed and elbowed by the melancholy Sunday crowds. . . . Just about now, Yves Frontenac must be driving that way in his saloon car. What it must cost to eat the sort of things one saw on the side-tables of fashionable restaurants – the crayfish, and the peaches in their padded boxes, and those things that looked like over-sized lemons! How much, she would never know. She had always, herself, been confined to

a choice between one or other of the cheap table-d'hôtes –
3 fr. 50, all in. . . . She looked towards the West, and thought
of Yves Frontenac in the company of a lady and another young
man.

Dinner was almost over. She had got up, and was making
her way between the tables, saying that she had got to do something about her face. Yves made a sign to the wine-waiter to
serve the champagne. He seemed to be quite calm: the tense-
ness had gone from his manner. All through the meal Geo had
been engaged in giving the young woman the information she
wanted on the subject of cabin-trunks and dressing-cases (he
knew a man who could get them for her at wholesale prices).
It was quite clear that they were not going to be of the
same party. Everything they said pointed, on the contrary,
to the fact that they were going to be away from each
other for several months, and were facing the prospect with
equanimity.

"They're playing that bit of nonsense that was all the rage
two years ago," said Geo.

He started humming with the orchestra – "*Non, tu ne
saurais jamais . . .*"

"Geo, you can have no idea what a fool I've been. . . ."

Yves looked at the friendly face of the young man, whose
hand, as he raised his glass, was trembling slightly. His eyes
were shining.

"I thought you were going away with her, that you were
trying to keep me in the dark."

Geo gave a shrug and fingered his tie. It was an habitual
gesture with him. Then he opened a black-enamel case, and
took a cigarette. His eyes never left Yves's face.

"When I think of you, Yves, with all you've got in
there" (and he touched his friend's forehead with a nicotine-

stained finger) . . . "of you, and this . . . I don't want to be offensive . . ."

"Oh, don't mind me! I know you think she's a little fool – still, preaching doesn't sit very well on you."

"I," said Geo, "am a nobody."

He leaned his charming, rather worn face, slightly forward, raised it again, and smiled at Yves with an expression of affection and admiring respect.

"Besides, I'm not likely to let myself be caught again, until . . ."

He made a sign to the wine-waiter, emptied his glass, and, with a rather wild look in his eyes, gave an order:

"Two brandies . . . You see all these stylish tarts," he went on, "well, I'd give the whole boiling for . . . guess what?"

He leaned forward, and looked across the table with his magnificent eyes. In a tone that was at once ashamed and passionate, he murmured:

"For the little girl who does the washing-up!"

They burst out laughing. Suddenly, a whole world of sadness clamped down on Yves. He looked across at Geo who, like himself, had become gloomy. Was his friend, he wondered, also conscious of this feeling that everything was a hollow, an unending, mockery? Far, far away, beyond immeasurable distances, he thought that he could hear the drowsy murmur of the pines.

"Uncle Xavier . . ." he muttered.

"What did you say?"

Geo put down his glass and signed to the wine-waiter, with forefinger raised, to bring another brandy.

XIX

ONE morning in October, Joséfa found herself standing in the entrance-hall of the d'Orsay Hotel, surrounded by the Frontenac children (with the single exception of José, who was still in Morocco). Their uncle's condition had seemed to be improving during the summer, but a more than usually violent attack had recently laid him low, and the doctor had little hope that he would recover. Joséfa's telegram had been delivered at Respide, where Yves was superintending the wine-harvest, and already thinking about returning to Paris. He was in no hurry to do so, since "she" would not be back until the end of the month. Besides, he had grown used to being away from her, and, now that he was within sight of the exit from the tunnel, would willingly have dawdled.

Intimidated by the presence of so many Frontenacs, Joséfa had at first taken refuge behind a wall of dignity. But her feelings had been too much for her, and she had found it impossible to maintain her carefully considered attitude. Besides, Jean-Louis had found his way to her heart with his very first words. Her worship of the Frontenacs had at last been rewarded. Here was someone who would not disappoint her. It was to him now, as head of the family, that she addressed herself. . . . The two young women were standing rather rigidly aloof, not, as Joséfa thought, out of haughtiness, but because they had not yet made up their minds what attitude they ought to adopt. (She would never have thought they could be such strapping wenches. They appeared to have monopolized all the family ration of fat). Yves, who was always dead-beat after a night journey, had ensconced himself in an armchair.

"I told him that I would pass myself off to you as his house-keeper. Since he never speaks at all now (it's not because he won't but because he's afraid it might bring on an attack), I can't say for sure whether he agreed or not. There are times when his poor mind seems to wander . . . it's difficult to know what he wants . . . the truth of the matter is that he's thinking all the time about that there pain which may return at any moment . . . something dreadful it is, seemingly . . . like as he had a mountain on his chest. . . . I only hope as you'll never see him when he's bad. . . ."

"It must be terrible for you, madame. . . ."

She spluttered through her tears:

"What a kind heart you have, Monsieur Jean-Louis!"

"But at least, in all his bad times, he has had the support of your love and devotion."

Conventional though the words were, they had on Joséfa the effect of an endearment. She had suddenly become one of the family, and stood there crying quietly, her hand clinging to Jean-Louis's arm. Marie whispered in Danièle's ear:

"It was very wrong of him to spend so much money: we shall never get things straight."

It was agreed that Joséfa should prepare their uncle for their coming. They would turn up about ten, and wait outside the front door.

It was only on the squalid landing, where the Frontenac children stood listening, while the other tenants, put wise by the concierge, leaned inquisitive faces over the banisters: it was only when he was sitting on the dirty stone stair, with his back leaning against the scarred surface of the imitation marble, that Yves at last realized the full horror of what was going on behind that closed door. Every now and then Joséfa opened it just wide enough to give passage to her puffy, tear-stained face, and

begged them to wait a little longer. Then, putting a finger to
her lips, she shut it again. Uncle Xavier, who once every fortnight had entered the gloomy room in the rue de Cursol in
Bordeaux, after making his round of the family estates; Uncle
Xavier, who could cut a whistle from an alder-twig, was now
lying at death's door in the awful slum where this woman
lived, just opposite the railway bridge, and not far from the
La Motte-Picquet-Grenelle station. Poor man, bound hand and
foot by prejudices and phobias, incapable of going back on any
opinion that he had inherited, inalterably, from his parents, so
great a respecter of the established order, yet such a stranger
to any simple and normal way of life. . . .

The smell that filled the stair-well brought back the very
atmosphere of the house in the rue de Cursol, as Yves had
known it when term began, and he had returned there from
the country. It was a smell made up of fog, and damp pave-
ments, and linoleum. Danièle and Marie were whispering.
Jean-Louis was standing motionless with closed eyes, his forehead pressed to the wall. Yves made no attempt to speak to
him, realizing that his brother was praying. "It is you, Monsieur Jean-Louis," Joséfa had said, "who will have to speak
to him of the Good God. He would jump down my throat
if *I* so much as tried!" Yves would have liked to follow his
example, but his tongue had lost the feel of those forgotten
words. It was a far, far call to the distant days when he, too,
had only to close his eyes and clasp his hands. . . . How long
the time seemed! He knew by heart all the patterns made by
the stains on the stairs where he was squatting.

Once more Joséfa pushed the door ajar, and this time she
made a sign to them to enter. She showed them into the dining-
room and vanished. The Frontenacs held their breath, and
scarcely dared to move, because Jean-Louis's boots creaked.
The window must have been shut since the evening before.

The stale smells of food and gas had accumulated between these four red-papered walls. The two colour-prints, one of peaches, the other of raspberries, were identical with just such another pair which had once hung in the dining-room at Preignac.

Only later did they realize that they ought not to have gone in all together. If he had first seen only Jean-Louis, their uncle might have grown used to the idea of their presence. It was madness to have crowded in together.

"Here they are, sir," Joséfa said, doing her best to play her chosen part of housekeeper: " – it's a great happiness for you, sir, isn't it, to have them with you? . . . They've all come, except Monsieur José."

Not a move did he make, but sat in the grip of a reptilian immobility. . . . In that terrible face, only the eyes slid from side to side, shifting from one to another of them, as though some threatened blow were about to fall. His two hands clung to his coat, pressed hard against his panting chest. Suddenly, Joséfa forgot her part:

"You won't speak because you're afraid it might do you a hurt, is that it? All right, ducky, don't you say nothing if you'd rather not. You can see them, can't you? – and it makes you happy. Look as much as you like, but don't speak a word. If you come over queer, just you tell me, my pet. If you're in pain, just make a sign. Want your injection, is that it? I'll go and get it ready."

So she lulled and comforted him in such words as one uses to the very young. But the dying man, still tense, still watchful, retained his haunted look. The four Frontenacs, standing in a tight bunch, rigid with anguish, were unaware that they looked just like members of a jury about to be sworn in. At last, Jean-Louis, breaking from the group, laid his arm about his uncle's shoulder.

"Only José's failed to turn up on parade, you see: but the latest news of him is good."

Xavier Frontenac's lips moved. They all of them leaned above his chair, but could not, at first, make out what he was saying.

"Who told you to come?"

"Madame . . . your housekeeper."

"She . . . is . . . not . . . my . . . housekeeper. Understand that: not . . . my . . . housekeeper. You heard how she spoke to me. . . ."

Yves knelt down close to the skinny legs.

"What does it matter, Uncle Xavier? . . . it's of no import-ance whatever . . . it doesn't concern us. You are our beloved uncle, our father's brother. . . ."

But the sick man, with averted eyes, pushed him away. "You know now! . . . you know now! . . ." he kept on saying with a wild look in his eyes. "I am like Uncle Péloueyre. He shut himself away at Bourideys, I remember, with that woman of his . . . wouldn't see any of the family. . . . Your father . . . who was a very young man, then . . . was deputed to go and see him. . . . I recall how Michel set off on horseback, with a joint, because his uncle liked our Preignac mutton. . . . Your father described how he stood there, knocking at the door. . . . At last Uncle Péloueyre opened it a crack . . . stared at Michel . . . took the joint . . . shut the door and bolted it. . . . I remember his telling us about it . . . it's an odd story . . . but I'm talking too much . . . a very odd story."

He began to laugh in a sort of suppressed and concentrated fashion. He could not stop though the laughter aggravated his condition. A fit of coughing shook him.

Joséfa came back and gave him his injection. He closed his eyes. A quarter of an hour went by. The noise of the trains set the house shaking. When they had passed, nothing could be heard but his terrible, gasping struggle for breath. Suddenly he stirred in his chair, and opened his eyes.

"Are Marie and Danièle here? They will have been in the house of my mistress. I shall have been the cause of their seeing the woman whom I keep. If Blanche and Michel could have known that, they would have cursed me. I have brought Michel's children into the house of my mistress!"

That was all he said. His nose had a pinched look: his face was blue. Raucous sounds came from him, that terrible noise of gurgling which means the end. . . . Joséfa, her eyes streaming with tears, took him in her arms, while the Frontenacs withdrew in terror towards the door.

"You don't need to feel ashamed with them, ducky . . . they're good, they are, they know about things, they understand. . . . What is it? . . . what do you want, my poor chickabiddy?"

In sudden panic she turned towards the children:

"What is he saying? I can't make out what he's saying!"

They could see only too well what that movement of his arm from left to right meant: it meant "Go away!" God would not let her understand that he was dismissing her, his companion of so many years, his only friend, his servant and his wife.

In the darkness, the noise of the last train smothered her groans. She abandoned herself, without restraint, to her grief, feeling the need to cry aloud. The concierge and the daily woman held her by the arms, and dabbed at her temples with vinegar. The Frontenac children had fallen to their knees.

XX

"AND what surprises have you in store for us, now?" Dussol intended the question to be friendly, though he could not suppress a smile.

Yves, curled up on Jean-Louis's divan, pretended that he had not heard. He was to take the night train to Paris. It was late in the afternoon, two days after Uncle Xavier's funeral at Preignac. Dussol, who had not been able to be present (he was a victim, now, to rheumatism, and for the last year had been able to walk only with the help of two sticks), had come to pay his respects to the family.

"I imagine," he said, "that you've got something on the stocks?"

The light had not been switched on, and he could barely see Yves's face. The young man was still silent.

"What a young slyboots you are! Come, now, out with it! . . . fish or flesh? verse or prose?"

At that, Yves made up his mind:

"I'm writing a collection of 'Characters' . . . taken from nature. . . . No merit, I can assure you . . . I have invented nothing . . . merely reproduced most of the types I have come across in the course of my life."

"What is it going to be called? just *Characters*?"

"No: *Mugs*."

There was a moment's silence. Madeleine turned to Dussol, and, in a choking voice, said: "Do let me give you another cup?" Jean-Louis asked something about an important felling operation near Bourideys, for which the Frontenac-Dussol firm was negotiating.

"It's not your fault, I know," said Dussol: "all the same, it's

167

a nuisance that your uncle's death has delayed the conclusion of the deal. Lacagne's in the field, you know. . . ."

"I'm meeting him the day after tomorrow, early, on the site. . . ."

Jean-Louis spoke absent-mindedly. Most of his attention was being given to Yves, whose forehead and hands alone were visible. He got up and turned on the light. Yves half averted his head, revealing to his brother's eyes a crop of tousled brown hair, a hollow, pallid cheek, and the graceful line of his neck.

"I've half a mind to go back to Paris with Yves," Jean-Louis said on the spur of the moment. "I must see Labat . . ."

"But in that case you wouldn't be back in time for your meeting the day after tomorrow," Dussol protested: "Labat can go hang! D'you realize that there's profit in this Bourideys' felling to the tune of a hundred thousand francs?"

Jean-Louis passed his hand over his nose and mouth. Why this sudden feeling of terror – this idea that he mustn't let Yves out of his sight for a single moment?

As soon as Dussol had left, he went into the bedroom. Madeleine followed him.

"Is it because of Yves?" she asked. She had learned to see into her husband's mind, and he knew it. He felt that she could read him like a book.

"I don't mind admitting that I'm worried about him."

She tried to argue. It was all nonsense, really it was. Yves had been upset by Uncle Xavier's death. A few days in Paris would soon put him right.

"We know the kind of way he lives. . . . He keeps the gloomy moods for his family, with the result that you start worrying. From what Dussol's been able to discover, he is not usually regarded as a wet blanket by his friends. Surely you're not going to risk the loss of a hundred thousand francs, just for something that's probably got no existence except in your imagination?"

Instinctively, she had put her finger on the one argument that was always effective with Jean-Louis. It wasn't only his money that was in question, but the family's. For the rest of the evening, he did his best to keep up a conversation with his brother, who seemed perfectly calm, and answered his questions without even raising his voice. There was nothing to justify Jean-Louis's anxiety. All the same, he very nearly did not get out of the railway carriage in which he had installed Yves, when the porter came along shutting the doors.

As soon as they were through the Lormont tunnels, Yves felt that he could breathe more freely. He was on his way back to "her". Each turn of the wheels helped to shorten the distance between them. They had agreed to meet at eleven o'clock next morning in an underground bar, at the corner of one of the Avenues, close to the Etoile. This time he was expecting the worst, and so was armed against disappointment. No matter what she might say or do, he was about to see her again. So long as he had something to look forward to, some meeting arranged for, he could go on living. But he must make his times of seeing her more frequent than they had been during the year just past. He would say: "I find myself gasping for breath rather sooner than I used to. You mustn't expect me to remain out of water for too long. In you I live, and breathe and have my being." She would smile. She knew that Yves had no particular liking for travellers' tales, and would cut short what she had to tell him about the cruise. 'I will make her understand that human geography is the only geography I find interesting: that it's not the views she's seen that I care about, but the people she's met in the course of these three months. No doubt there'll turn out to have been fewer of them than I think. . . . She says there's nothing more important in her life than me. Nevertheless, she's surrounded by adoring males. . . . Who was it she was going about with last year? . . .' He fumbled about with his feet for the bloodstained tracks which lay across the last twelve months. He scratched at himself like a leper, waking old jealousies, making old scabs bleed again. He was rushing on towards a city which had nothing in common with the Paris in which, only one week ago, Xavier Frontenac had died so horribly.

"Darling, *must* you look at your watch? We've been together for exactly ten minutes, and already you're worrying about the time. You just live for the moment when I shan't be with you!"

"Can't we have a little let-up from complaints and reproaches? . . . Tell me, do you think I'm looking brown?"

He thought it tactful to praise her suit and her fox-fur. She was duly pleased. He let her go on for quite a while about the Balearic Islands. Still, on three separate occasions, he had already made her say that she had met no one of any interest to her – except her former husband, whom she had run into in Marseilles. They had had lunch together, like a couple of old friends. . . . He was becoming more and more wedded to his drugs, and had had to hurry away to get a pipe of opium . . . just couldn't do without it.

"And what about you, Yves, my pet?"

All the time he was speaking she was busy with her face, reddening her lips, dabbing her cheeks with powder. When he told her about Uncle Xavier's death, she asked, without any particular show of interest, whether it would make any "difference" to him.

"He had made over most of his fortune to us in his lifetime."

"Then there's nothing particularly exciting about his death, is there?"

There was no spitefulness in the words. . . . He'd have to

start on a whole string of explanations . . . introduce her into a whole world of memories, a universe of mystery. . . . A woman joined the young man who had been sitting alone at the table opposite. They kissed. There were two or three men sitting at the bar. None of them turned round. Motor-buses were rumbling up the Avenue. The electric lights were on. There was nothing to show that it was morning. She was eating cold potato-chips, one by one.

"I'm hungry," she said.

"Lunch any good to you? . . . when can we make a date? – tomorrow? . . ."

"Let me think . . . tomorrow? . . . four o'clock I've got a fitting . . . six . . . no, not tomorrow . . . how about Thursday?"

"Three days from now?" he said, and his voice sounded indifferent. Three days and three nights out of her life about which he would know nothing, days and nights filled with people who were strangers to him, with incidents which would remain for ever hidden from him. . . . He had believed himself to be prepared for just such a situation, had thought he would feel no surprise. But pain is unforeseeable. For months and months he had grown breathless in pursuit of her. Three months' pause, and here was the old dance beginning all over again. But the circumstances were different now. He was all-in, done up. He wouldn't be able to stick the pace. She realized that he was suffering, and took his hand. He did not withdraw it. She asked him what he was thinking about. He said:

"I was thinking of Respide. The other day, after my uncle's funeral, I went there alone from Preignac. My brother had gone straight back to Bordeaux, with my sisters. I had the house opened up for me. I went into the drawing-room. It was full of damp-rot and smelled of mould and decaying floor-boards. The shutters were closed. . . . I lay down at full length on the chintz sofa in the half-light. I could feel the coldness of the wall against my cheek. I shut my eyes and tried to imagine that I was lying there between my mother and my uncle. . . ."

"Yves, you do say the most abominable things! . . ."

"Never had I so completely succeeded in getting into the very skin of death. The walls were thick, the room like some cavern hidden away at the heart of that remote estate . . . night . . . and all around me, life stretching to infinity. . . . I was at peace . . . peace, darling, think of that! . . . finished with the urgency of love . . . Why are we always taught to dread annihilation? . . . The really awful thing is to believe, against all evidence, in life eternal! To live eternally would be to lose the refuge of nothingness."

He saw that she was furtively glancing at her wrist-watch. She said:

"Yves, I really must rush. . . . We'd better not be seen leaving together. Thursday, then? . . . Shall we say seven o'clock at my place? . . . no, half-past . . . no, better make it a quarter to eight. . . ."

"No," said he, laughing: "it shall be eight o'clock!"

XXI

Y VES was still laughing as he walked down the Champs-Elysées. There was nothing forced or bitter about his laughter. The sound was so frank and so free that people turned to look at him. . . . It was only just after noon, and he had climbed the stairs from the d'Orsay station in the early hours of the morning. In that brief space of time he had drained to the dregs the delight of seeing her again to which he had been looking forward for three whole months. And now, here he was, wandering the streets. . . . It really was a "scream", as she was so fond of saying. The gay mood was still with him as he dropped on to a bench at the Rond-Point. He felt as much done up as though he had walked all the way from his native heaths. He was conscious of no pain, but only of a feeling of exhaustion. Never had the object of his love seemed to him so utterly worthless as now, when he had been kicked out of her life and trodden under foot, as now, when he was fouled and finished. Nevertheless, his love was still there. It was like a mill, grinding away – on nothing. He had stopped laughing now. His mind withdrew into itself, concentrating upon this strange torment in a non-existent world. He was living through those moments known to all lovers when, with arms still clasped across their breasts, as though what they have been embracing has not really vanished, they strain to their hearts, quite literally – nothing. On this mild, warm noon of October, seated on a bench at the Rond-Point des Champs-Elysées, the last of the Frontenacs could see no future of any kind waiting for him beyond the Chevaux de Marly. Once past *them*, he could not say, for the life of him, whether he would turn to right or left, or go straight on to the Tuileries and enter the mouse-trap of the Louvre.

All around him cars and people swirled and mingled, breaking into different streams at the meeting-place of the Avenues. He felt as utterly alone as he had done once in that narrow clearing, walled in with furze and bracken, where, in his untamed childhood, he had loved to hide. The unbroken roar of the streets sounded to him like the sweet boisterousness of Nature, and the passers-by seemed stranger in his eyes than the pines of Bourideys, the summits of which had once looked down at a tiny Frontenac snuggling at their feet in a thickness of underbrush. Today, these men and women were like flies above the heather, like hovering dragonflies. Now and again, one of them would settle at his side, rub against his sleeve, then, without even seeing him, take flight again. How muffled, now, and distant had that voice become which once had followed this young Frontenac into his secret hut. But, however muted, he could hear it still. Now he could clearly see – so said the voice – all the obstructed paths which once had been foretold, the passions from which there could be no escape. . . . Better turn back . . . turn in his tracks. . . . But how is it possible to turn in one's tracks when strength is spent? To trudge back all that way? – what a climb! and what was there waiting at the end of it? Yves was a wanderer now upon the earth, freed from all human labour. No work was demanded of him. He had finished his task before the hour struck, had handed in his fair copy, and gone off to play. His only occupation was to note, day by day, the reactions of a mind wholly without employment. He could have done no more, and the world demanded no more of him. Which, among the thousands of tasks that set these human ants swarming about his bench, could have served his purpose? Ah, better far to die of hunger. . . . "Yet, you know well," the voice insisted, "that you were created to carry through an exhausting labour, and to that labour you would have submitted, body and soul, because it would not have turned you from the deep-running life of love. That is the one form of work in all the world which would in no wise have diverted you from love, which, at every moment, would have made love manifest and joined you to all men in charity. . . ." Yves shook his head, and cried: "Oh, dear God, let me be!"

He got up, and walked the short distance to the Metro entrance, close to the Grand Palais. He leaned upon the balustrade. It was the hour when the work-rooms all fill up again, when the Metro sucks in and vomits forth a crowd of ants with human faces. For a long while, Yves, with fascinated gaze, followed this ingurgitation, this spewing out, of human creatures. A day was coming – he felt sure of it, and, from the depths of his despair and weariness, he called upon it – when all men and women would be forced to obey this tidal rhythm, all, without one single exception. What Jean-Louis called the "social question" would be present no longer to the finer spirits among mankind. . . . Yves thought: 'I must live to see that day when the lock-gates will open and close at stated intervals before the human flood. When that time comes, no inherited fortune will make it possible for any Frontenac to stand aloof on pretext of thinking, of indulging in despair, of writing a Journal, of praying, of achieving a personal salvation. The people of the lower depths will have triumphed over all human values. Yes, the human being, as such, will have been destroyed, and with his destruction will have disappeared that torment and that dear delight which we call love. No longer will those lunatics exist who can see infinity within the finite. What joy to think that the time may be close at hand when all the Frontenacs – for want of air that they can breathe – will have vanished from the earth: when no creature will exist who can even imagine what I, at this moment, am feeling, as I lean upon this Metro balustrade – this stale sickness of sentiment, this over-chewed cud of brooding on what *she*, since first I knew her, may have said to make me believe that she still clings to me – as the sick man, from among the many things his doctor may have said, isolates just those which once gave him hope, which now he knows by heart (but no longer have they any power over him, dwell on them though he may . . .)

Beyond the Chevaux de Marly he could see nothing more to do than lay him down and sleep. Death had no meaning for him, poor sad immortal. On that side the road was barred. A Frontenac knows that into nothingness no way leads out, and that a guard has been set at the door of the tomb. In the world he was imagining, the world he saw, and felt must come, no man would be haunted by the temptation of death, because the human race of that future date, weighed down by lives laborious and filled with busyness, will seem alive but be already dead. For to have the choice between life and death, a man must be an individual, different from other men, bearing his own existence in his hands, capable of measuring its scope, of judging it with lucid glance beneath the watchful eye of God.

It amused him to think of these things. . . . He made a promise to himself that he would tell Jean-Louis all he had been thinking as he had hung above the entrance to the Metro. What fun it would be to see his brother's surprised face, as Yves described to him the nature of that revolution to come which would be accomplished in the secret places of the heart, achieving a dissociation in man's nature, so that, in the end, he would be turned into something resembling one of the hymenoptera – a bee, an ant. . . . No centuries-old park would ever again stretch branches over one single and continuing family. The pine-trees on the old estates would not in future watch, year after year, always the same children grow, nor, in the thin, pure faces gazing upwards at their crests, recognize the features of their fathers and their grandfathers before them. . . . It was because he was so tired, thought Yves, that his mind was wandering like this. How wonderful it would be to sleep! The question now for him was not of life or death, but only of sleep. He hailed a taxi, and, as he drove, fingered in his pocket a tiny bottle. He held it close to his eyes. It was pure pleasure to decipher on its label the magic formula: *Allylisopropylacetylurea c̄ phenyldimethylpyrazolone ā ā*, gr 1·6.

All through those same hours, Jean-Louis, seated opposite Madeleine at table, standing, while he hastily swallowed his coffee, at the wheel of his car, in his office, as he sat watching his clerk Janin who was making a report to him, kept on saying to himself – 'Yves is not in danger: I've no reason whatever to be anxious. Yesterday evening in the train he seemed calmer than I have seen him for a long time . . . that's what worries me . . . that calmness . . .' From somewhere in the docks he could hear the puffing of a locomotive. Why should he let this business appointment keep him from going? – he could explain it all to Janin. Here he was in the room with him: a man with plenty of initiative, and passionately anxious to get his chance. Already his bright, observant eyes were trying to make out what Jean-Louis was thinking, to get just one step ahead of him . . . and quite suddenly, Jean-Louis knew with absolute certainty that he would start that night for Paris. By tomorrow he would be there. The knowledge brought back his peace of mind. It was as though the unknown power which, since the previous evening, had had him by the throat, now knew it could relax its grip, because he would obey.

XXII

FROM the bottom of a deep pit Yves could hear, infinitely far away, a bell ringing. The confused idea came to him that it was the telephone. Somebody was calling him from Bordeaux to say that his mother had been taken ill (though he knew she had been dead for more than a year). A short while ago she had been in this very room. She had visited it only once in her life (she had come from Bordeaux to see Yves. She had wanted, she said, to be able to visualize his surroundings when she thought of him). She had never come again – until last night. Yves could see her still, as he had seen her in the arm-chair by his bed, her hands idle, since she was dead. The dead can neither knit nor speak. . . . But her lips had moved. She had had something urgent to impart, but could not make her-self heard. She had come in, as she always used to do at Bourideys, when there was something on her mind, without knocking, just pressing the handle gently down, and pushing the door open with her body, lost in her preoccupation, not noticing that she might, perhaps, be interrupting him in his reading or his writing, in his sleep or in a fit of tears. . . . There she had stood, yet, somebody was telephoning from Bordeaux to tell him she was dead. He gazed at her in anguish, striving to catch upon her lips the *something* she wanted to say, and could not. . . . The ringing went on and on. What should he answer? Then the front door banged, and he heard the voice of the daily woman: "Lucky I've got a key. . . ." Then, the other voice, Jean-Louis's (but he's in Bordeaux) . . . "He looks very peaceful . . . he's sleeping quite quietly . . . no, the bottle's almost full, he can't have taken very much. . . ." Jean-Louis was in Bordeaux, but, at the same time, he was here, in this room. Yves gave him a reassuring smile:

"Hullo, old man . . ."

"What are you doing in Paris? . . ."

"Some business brought me up . . ."

Life flowed in on Yves from every side. Slowly it made its way in as the tide of sleep receded. . . . He remembered now: what cowardice! – three tablets! Jean-Louis was asking him what was wrong. Yves made no attempt to pretend. Pretence was beyond his powers: strength had drained from him like blood from a wound. All the circumstances of the time just past came suddenly to focus. Two days ago he had been in Bordeaux: yesterday morning, in the little bar. Then had followed those hours of madness . . . and now, here was Jean-Louis.

"But how did you manage to get away? . . . I thought this was the day of the big deal? . . ."

Jean-Louis shook his head. "A sick man mustn't worry his head over things like that."

And Yves:

"No, I'm not feverish – just knocked-up, all in. . . ."

Jean-Louis had taken his wrist, and now, with his eye on his watch, was counting the pulse-beats, as mamma used to do in the days of their childhood illnesses. Then, with a gesture – which also recalled their mother – the elder brother pushed the hair back from Yves's forehead, so as to make sure that he really was not feverish – perhaps, too, in order to reveal the younger man's face, to see his features clearly: and also, who knows? in a simple access of tenderness.

"Don't get agitated," said Jean-Louis: "don't talk."

"You'll stay with me, won't you?"

"Yes, I'll stay."

"Sit down: no, not on the bed: bring up the arm-chair."

Neither of them moved. The confused sounds of the autumn morning disturbed them not at all. Now and again, Yves, opening his eyes, saw his brother's serious, honest face marked with the strain and weariness of the night. Jean-Louis, freed from the anxious brooding which had been gnawing at him for the last two days, had yielded at last to the deep sense of peace which flowed over him as he sat beside the bed in which his younger brother lay alive and well. About noon, he ate a hurried meal without leaving the room. The day seemed to be running through his fingers like sand through an hour-glass. Suddenly, the telephone bell started to ring. . . . The sick man showed signs of restlessness. Jean-Louis laid his finger to his lips and slipped into the adjoining dressing-room. Yves had a happy feeling that everything now was out of his hands. It was for others to get him out of the mess. Jean-Louis would arrange everything.

". . . . Bordeaux? . . . that you, Dussol? . . . yes, it's me speaking . . . I can hear you . . . I can't help it . . . couldn't put off this trip. . . . No, Janin's acting for me . . . of course . . . he's got my instructions . . . well, it can't be helped . . . yes, I know . . . more than a hundred thousand francs . . . just too bad. . . ."

"He's hung up," said Jean-Louis, coming back into the bedroom.

He sat down again by the bed. Yves began to question him. Was it because of him that the deal about which Dussol had been speaking had misfired? His brother reassured him. He had taken all the necessary steps before leaving. It was a good sign that Yves was showing anxiety, that he wanted to know, for instance, whether Joséfa had got the cheque which they had decided to send her.

"Would you believe it, old man, she actually sent it back. . . ."

"I always said it wasn't enough. . . ."

"You're barking up the wrong tree. She sent it back because she thought it was too much. Uncle Xavier had given her a hundred thousand francs in hard cash. . . . She wrote me a letter in which she said that he had felt very guilty about the money, and couldn't get the idea out of his mind that he had deprived *us* of it. She doesn't want to do anything that might be contrary to his wishes. All the poor creature asks is to be allowed to send us her good wishes each New Year's day. She says she hopes I will let her have news of the family and that I will advise her about her investments."

"What securities did Uncle Xavier buy for her?"

"*Lombards Anciens* and *Noblesse Russe*, three and a half per cent. There's nothing for her to worry about. . . ."

"Is she living at Niort with her daughter?"

"Yes . . . and, oh, by the way, she wants to keep our photographs. Marie and Danièle don't quite like the idea, but she has promised not to display them, but to keep them in the glass-fronted wardrobe. . . . What do you think?"

It was Jean-Louis's opinion that the humble Joséfa had entered into the Frontenac mystery, and now formed part of it. Nothing, he thought, from now on, could break her connexion with it. Beyond any doubt, she was entitled to her photographs and to her New Year's wishes. . . .

"Look here, Jean-Louis, when José has finished his military service, I'm all for our living together, snuggling up like puppies in a basket. . . ." (He knew that this could never be.)

"Like when we used to put our napkins on our heads, and play at 'Communities', in the small room, remember?"

"How extraordinary to think that that room still exists. Life marches on . . . but Bourideys, at least, hasn't changed."

"A lot of timber has been cut," said Jean-Louis. . . . "In the Lassus direction there's been quite a clean sweep . . . and all along the road, too. . . . Try to imagine the mill, with not a tree standing. . . ."

"There'll always be the pines in the park."

"They're rotting where they stand. . . . Every year a few of them die."

Yves sighed:

"The Frontenac pines, wearing away like human flesh and blood."

"Yves, what d'you say to our going back to Bourideys together?"

Yves made no reply. He was trying to remember what Bourideys would be looking like at that moment. The evening breeze must be clashing the high tops of the pines together, then tearing them apart, then once more making a tangle of their branches, as though the shackled trees had private things to say to one another, and secrets to shower upon the earth. . . . After the shower, the forest would be filled with the sound of rain-drops. . . . They would go out upon the terrace to sniff the autumn evening. . . . But, if Bourideys, for Yves, existed still, it was only as his mother, while he lay dreaming, had existed. She had seemed to be living, though he knew her to be dead. In Bourideys today nothing was left but the abandoned chrysalis of childhood and of love. How could he express such feelings even to the brother who dwelt so deeply in his heart? He protested lamely, that it would be difficult for them to remain long together.

"You couldn't wait until I was cured."

Jean-Louis did not ask – "cured of what?" (He knew that he should have phrased it, "cured of whom?") It amazed him to think that so many young and charming beings, like Yves, could know love only in the form of suffering. For them it is no more than a tormenting fantasy. . . . But to Jean-Louis love seemed a simple and an easy thing . . . yet, if God did not command his highest loyalty! . . . He was deeply fond of Madeleine, and took Communion every Sunday: yet, twice already, once with a girl in the office, once with one of his wife's friends, he had felt that a rather special link existed . . . had been conscious of something to which he was only too ready to respond. . . . He had had to pray hard, but even so was not at all sure that he had not been guilty of the sin of desire . . . for how is it always possible to distinguish temptation from desire? Holding his brother's hand in the lamplight, he gazed with sad surprise at the face so seamed with pain, at the clenched jaw, at all the tell-tale marks of exhaustion and fatigue.

Perhaps Yves would have been pleased if Jean-Louis had questioned him. But the shyness between them was too strong. Jean-Louis would have liked to say – "your work . . ." but to have done so would have been to risk wounding him. Besides, he felt confusedly, that his brother's work, if it were to flower into supreme achievement, must ever be the expression of despair. . . . He knew by heart the poem in which Yves, when little more than a child, had told how, if he were to be torn from silence, he would need, as did the pines of Bourideys, the wild West wind, and an infinity of torment.

Jean-Louis would have liked to say: "a home . . . a wife . . . other Frontenac children. . . ." Above all, he would have liked to speak to him of God, but dared not.

A little later (darkness had already fallen), he leaned over Yves, whose eyes were closed, and was surprised to see him smile, to hear him murmur that he was not asleep. Jean-Louis was rejoiced to see the tenderness and calm which lit the gaze that held his own so long. He would have liked to know what it was that Yves was thinking. He could not know that what produced that smile was the happiness Yves felt that he was not to die in solitude. No, never would he die alone. Wherever it might be that death would find him, he believed, he knew, that his elder brother would be with him, holding his hand, and going with him as far as it is possible for another human being to go, to the brink of the great darkness.

Far away, in the country of the Frontenacs and the Péloueyres, beyond the lost lands where the tracks end, the moon was shining on the drenched and spongy heath. It kept its state especially in that clearing of the trees, left free by the resinous growths, around some five or six huge oaks, very old and very gnarled, giant children of the earth. There it was still possible for the slashed and wounded pines to raise their heads Heavenwards. Drowsy sheep-bells were tinkling at intervals in the pastures, known as the "parc de l'Homme", where one of the Frontenac shepherds was spending the October darkness. But for the occasional cry of some prowling animal of the night, and the jolting of a passing wagon, no sound broke the murmur of the breeze as it passed on from pine to pine, from the distant brink of ocean, travelling along the dense network of their branches. Within the hut, empty of sportsmen till the dawn should break, blinded pigeons, set there as decoys, fluttered their wings and suffered pangs of thirst and hunger. A flight of cranes creaked its way across the lighter spaces of the sky. From within the dark mystery of the Téchoueyre marshes, with their reedy, turf-ringed pools, sounded the whirring flap of water-birds. Old Frontenacs and Péloueyres, waking from the sleep of death in that corner of the world, would have seen no sign of change. The old oaks, fed for two centuries on the secret juices of the soil, were enjoying, at this very moment, a second, and more ephemeral, life in the mind of a young man lying in a Paris room with his brother fondly watching him. It was under the shade of those trees, thought Yves, that a great pit should have been dug, and in it piled and jumbled the bodies of all the Frontenac wives and husbands, of the Frontenac brothers and uncles, of the Frontenac sons. Only thus could the family have won the solace of one vast embrace, could have been mixed for ever with that much-loved earth, could have lain at home in nothingness.

Around, bent all in the same direction by the sea-wind, and offering to the West their rain-black bark, the pines would ever reach towards the sky, and strain and stretch. Each would have its wound – different from the wounds of all the others (each one of us knows why he bleeds). And he, Yves Frontenac, like them, wounded, and rooted like them in the drifting sand, but a free being with full liberty to tear himself adrift, should he so wish, from the world of the living, had chosen vainly to moan, to stay as one in the confused tangle of the human forest. Yet all his gestures were of supplication, and all his cries were still addressed to somebody.

He remembered his mother's worn face on one September evening at Bourideys, and how her eyes had sought for God behind the topmost branches. "Tell me, Yves, you who know so much . . . do the spirits in Heaven still think of those they have left behind upon the earth?" Since she could not imagine a world in which her sons had ceased to be the very heart of her heart, Yves had promised her that all separate loves would be perfected in one perfect love, single and absolute. And now, tonight, after many years, the words which he had uttered for her comfort, came back into his memory. Jean-Louis was sleeping. The night lamp shed a glow upon his gracious face. Oh, bond of the divine! Oh, mark of God's parentage! Never would the Frontenac mystery know corruption, for it was one beam of the Eternal Love refracted through the prism of a Race. The impossible union of wives and husbands, of sons and brothers, would, before long, be consummated. The last pines of Bourideys would see moving, not at their feet along the ride that led to the Great Oak, but far above their highest branches, a mother and her five children now made for ever one.

MORE ABOUT PENGUINS, PELICANS
AND PUFFINS

For further information about books available from Penguins please write to Dept EP, Penguin Books Ltd, Harmondsworth, Middlesex UB7 ODA.

In the U.S.A.: For a complete list of books available from Penguins in the United States write to Dept DG, Penguin Books, 299 Murray Hill Parkway, East Rutherford, New Jersey 07073.

In Canada: For a complete list of books available from Penguins in Canada write to Penguin Books Canada Ltd, 2801 John Street, Markham, Ontario L3R 1B4.

In Australia: For a complete list of books available from Penguins in Australia write to the Marketing Department, Penguin Books Australia Ltd, P.O. Box 257, Ringwood, Victoria 3134.

In New Zealand: For a complete list of books available from Penguins in New Zealand write to the Marketing Department, Penguin Books (N.Z.) Ltd, Private Bag, Takapuna, Auckland 9.

In India: For a complete list of books available from Penguins in India write to Penguin Overseas Ltd, 706 Eros Apartments, 56 Nehru Place, New Delhi 110019.

A CHOICE OF PENGUINS

☐ **_Further Chronicles of Fairacre_ 'Miss Read'**   £3.95

Full of humour, warmth and charm, these four novels – _Miss Clare Remembers, Over the Gate, The Fairacre Festival_ and _Emily Davis_ – make up an unforgettable picture of English village life.

☐ **_Callanish_ William Horwood**   £1.95

From the acclaimed author of _Duncton Wood_, this is the haunting story of Creggan, the captured golden eagle, and his struggle to be free.

☐ **_Act of Darkness_ Francis King**   £2.50

Anglo-India in the 1930s, where a peculiarly vicious murder triggers 'A terrific mystery story . . . a darkly luminous parable about innocence and evil' – _The New York Times_. 'Brilliantly successful' – _Daily Mail_. 'Unputdownable' – _Standard_

☐ **_Death in Cyprus_ M. M. Kaye**   £1.95

Holidaying on Aphrodite's beautiful island, Amanda finds herself caught up in a murder mystery in which no one, not even the attractive painter Steven Howard, is quite what they seem . . .

☐ **_Lace_ Shirley Conran**   £2.95

Lace is, quite simply, a publishing sensation: the story of Judy, Kate, Pagan and Maxine; the bestselling novel that teaches men about women, and women about themselves. 'Riches, bitches, sex and jetsetters' locations – they're all there' – _Sunday Express_

A CHOICE OF PENGUINS

☐ **West of Sunset** Dirk Bogarde £1.95

'His virtues as a writer are precisely those which make him the most compelling screen actor of his generation,' is what *The Times* said about Bogarde's savage, funny, romantic novel set in the gaudy wastes of Los Angeles.

☐ **The Riverside Villas Murder** Kingsley Amis £1.95

Marital duplicity, sexual discovery and murder with a thirties backcloth: 'Amis in top form' – *The Times*. 'Delectable from page to page . . . effortlessly witty' – C. P. Snow in the *Financial Times*

☐ **A Dark and Distant Shore** Reay Tannahill £3.95

Vilia is the unforgettable heroine, Kinveil Castle is her destiny, in this full-blooded saga spanning a century of Victoriana, empire, hatreds and love affairs. 'A marvellous blend of *Gone with the Wind* and *The Thorn Birds*. You will enjoy every page' – *Daily Mirror*

☐ **Kingsley's Touch** John Collee £1.95

'Gripping . . . I recommend this chilling and elegantly written medical thriller' – *Daily Express*. 'An absolutely outstanding storyteller' – *Daily Telegraph*

☐ **The Far Pavilions** M. M. Kaye £4.95

Holding all the romance and high adventure of nineteenth-century India, M. M. Kaye's magnificent, now famous, novel has at its heart the passionate love of an Englishman for Juli, his Indian princess. 'Wildly exciting' – *Daily Telegraph*

A CHOICE OF PENGUINS

☐ *Bliss* **Jill Tweedie**   £2.95

When beautiful Lady Clare La Fontaine marries for money, she enters a glittering world of luxury and corruption and discovers the darker side of sexual politics in Jill Tweedie's blockbusting, bestselling new novel. 'Huge, vital and passionately written' – *Cosmopolitan*

☐ *Swag* **Elmore Leonard**   £1.95

A thriller by the author of *Stick* and *LaBrava* – America's new No. 1 writer: 'He's something special' – *The New York Times*. 'The hottest thriller writer in the U.S.' – *Time*

These books should be available at all good bookshops or newsagents, but if you live in the UK or the Republic of Ireland and have difficulty in getting to a bookshop, they can be ordered by post. Please indicate the titles required and fill In the form below.

NAME _____ BLOCK CAPITALS

ADDRESS _____

_____

_____

Enclose a cheque or postal order payable to The Penguin Bookshop to cover the total price of books ordered, plus 50p for postage. Readers in the Republic of Ireland should send £IR equivalent to the sterling prices, plus 67p for postage. Send to: The Penguin Bookshop, 54/56 Bridlesmith Gate, Nottingham, NG1 2GP.

You can also order by phoning (0602) 599295, and quoting your Barclaycard or Access number.

Every effort is made to ensure the accuracy of the price and availability of books at the time of going to press, but it is sometimes necessary to increase prices and in these circumstances retail prices may be shown on the covers of books which may differ from the prices shown in this list or elsewhere. This list is not an offer to supply any book.

This order service is only available to residents in the UK and the Republic of Ireland.

● ● ●